MW01135439

Three Days in Seattle

by

Debra Burroughs

Copyright © 2012 Debra Burroughs

All rights reserved.

ISBN:147522219X
ISBN-13: 978-1475222197

All rights reserved as permitted under the U.S. Copyright Act of 1976, no part of this publication may be reproduced, distributed, or transmitted in any form or by any means, or stored in a database or retrieval system, without the prior permission of the publisher.

This is a work of fiction. Names, characters, places and incidents either are the product of the author's imagination or are used fictitiously. And any resemblance to actual persons, living, dead (or in any other form), business establishments, events, or locales is entirely coincidental.

Lake House Books
Boise, Idaho

2nd eBook Edition: 2014
2nd Paperback Edition: 2014

THREE DAYS IN SEATTLE by Debra Burroughs, 2nd. ed. p.cm.

Visit My Blog: www.DebraBurroughsBooks.com

Contact Me: Debra@DebraBurroughsBooks.com

DEDICATION

This book is dedicated to my amazing husband, Tim,

as well as to my awesome Beta Readers,

Buffy Drewett, Cathy Tomlinson,

and Janet Lewis.

TABLE OF CONTENTS

PROLOGUE

Whitney stirred from a deep sleep, waking to find herself in pitch-black darkness, her hands and feet bound. She yanked against the ropes, but the bonds were fastened to something solid.

Her head pounded, and she could only get air through her nose in short gasps. Something covered her mouth. Duct tape? She didn't know or care, she just needed air.

She struggled to scream, but the only sound she could make was a high-pitched moan.

Where am I? What's happening to me? Murky thoughts slogged through her disoriented mind. *Maybe I'm dreaming*, she thought. *Wake up, wake up, wake up!* But it was not a dream.

The sound of something scraping the floor made her freeze. She tried to listen, hear if someone or something was coming, but her heart thudding in her ears made it hard to concentrate.

A door creaked open, and she blinked as the harsh light hit her eyes. Was someone coming to rescue her? Or was it her captor? She decided not to risk it and shut her eyes, going limp, and hoped her pounding heart would not give her away.

CHAPTER 1

"IT'S VANCE ON THE PHONE AGAIN, Kate," the photographer's young assistant announced, holding out the cell phone to her.

Kate's chest tightened at the very mention of that man. She stood up and lowered her camera. "I'm in the middle of a photo shoot, Claire."

"It's the third time he's called today."

Kate looked down at the phone and assumed Vance could hear her response. "Tell him I'm working and can't talk."

Working or not, she didn't want to talk to him. Kate glanced over at the models, who she was sure were glaring at her for the delay. Then, pushing her long blonde hair over one shoulder, she turned back to her assistant. "Please, just take a message."

By the time the photo shoot was over, it was late, as evidenced by the table strewn with empty take-out boxes and coffee cups. They had worked through dinner, and the sun had long ago set over the Los Angeles area.

"I'm headed home," Claire said, tugging her jacket on as she walked across the spacious loft studio toward Kate, who was seated in front of her thirty-two-inch computer monitor, scanning through the day's shots. "You should call it a day too—you look beat."

Kate swiveled around in her chair and covered her yawn with her hand. "I'm not quite done, but I am tired." She'd arrived at the studio before eight a.m. and had been on her feet most of the day.

"I didn't tell you, but Vance called again about an hour ago."

"Thanks for taking care of him for me. He just won't take no for an answer." Kate leaned back in her chair and gathered her hair up into a ponytail.

She had been engaged to Vance Kerrigan, a handsome and successful Hollywood talent agent, until she discovered he had been cheating on her several months ago. She had called off the wedding and returned the ring, against his protests, and he continued to pursue her.

"I don't understand why you don't get a restraining order against him."

"Perhaps I should. I think he's been following me."

"What makes you think that?"

"You know that weird feeling you get when you think you're being watched?"

"Uh-huh."

"I keep getting that eerie sensation that someone's watching me, following me."

"That would creep me out," Claire said.

"I did tell a cop friend of mine who patrols my neighborhood. He's been driving past my condo now and then, keeping an eye out."

"That's not enough. You need to get a restraining order." Claire cocked her head and raised an eyebrow as if to say, *you need to listen to me.* "Why don't you get your things, and we can walk down to our cars together."

~*~

"Forget it, Vance! It's been a very long day, and I don't have the energy to argue with you. Please, stop calling me." Kate McAllister clicked off her cell phone and set it on the bathroom vanity. The last thing she wanted to think about right now was her two-timing ex-fiancé asking her to take him back.

The warm water in the claw-foot tub beckoned. She had been anticipating being enveloped by its warmth, letting it soothe away the stress of the day. Sticking one painted toe in the water, she checked the temperature before getting in. *Perfect*, she sighed softly.

As she was about to drop her fluffy white robe to the floor, the cell phone shrilled. "Shoot," she muttered under her breath. "If that's Vance again, I'm going to kill him."

A slight frown creased her brow as she turned and glanced at the Caller ID. She recognized the area code for Seattle, where her baby sister Whitney lived, but if it were her sister, the phone would have shown her name and not *Unknown Caller*.

Peering up at the wall clock, she saw the time was ten-forty-five pm. *Why would someone I don't know be calling me this late?* Tension crept up the back of her neck. *No one calls this late just to chat.* Reluctantly, she picked up the phone.

"Hello?"

"Kate, this is Suki. I'm sorry to call you so late." The woman on the other end of the line rattled on, "But, I, well, I need to—"

"Whoa. Slow down. You said your name is Suki?" Kate questioned.

"Yes, you know, Whitney's roommate."

"Oh, yes, sorry. I didn't recognize your name. Now, slow down and tell me – what's wrong, Suki?"

"Whitney's gone missing."

"What? When?" Panic began to set in. Kate's thoughts flew like a flock of spooked sparrows. Gathering herself, she tried to focus. Ordinarily, she connected with Whitney every day or two, but she had been so busy with work lately that Kate was ashamed to admit she did not notice when she hadn't heard from her sister recently.

"She's been missing since last night. Well, no, today. I mean, well, I didn't realize until this morning that she hadn't come home last night."

"Maybe she just stayed overnight at a friend's house." Whitney was twenty-four years old. She could stay out all night if she wanted to. Kate hoped that was all it was. The idea her sister could really be missing made her feel sick in the pit of her stomach.

"No, no, I don't think so, really. I think she would have told me so. We try to keep each other safe that way, you know. I have such a bad feeling about this, Kate. I think you should come to Seattle right away."

"You mean, like right now?" This news was all so unexpected. Frantic thoughts swirling in Kate's mind made it hard to process.

"Well, yeah. I mean, as soon as you can, of course."

"So, what do the police say?" Kate asked, searching for a voice of reason.

"Police?"

"Yes, Suki. You did call them, didn't you?" Kate was incredulous that her sister might be in danger and the police had not yet been informed. *Are you kidding me?* Her heart beat hard against her chest, sending pulsing blood painfully racing to her head.

"I'm sorry, Kate, don't get mad. I think you have to wait twenty-four hours before you can report someone missing, don't you?"

"How should I know, Suki? I would have called them to find out, not just assumed." A muscle twitched in Kate's jaw.

"You're right, you're right. I'm sorry."

"I'll call them for myself as soon as we get off the phone. I want to talk to the police before I come running up there." *Suki had all day to call me, why did she wait until now? Was she hoping Whitney would eventually show up? Something doesn't feel right.*

Perhaps Whitney was just staying over with a new boyfriend that Suki didn't know about. Or maybe she went with some girlfriends for a long weekend. *Suki is probably just overreacting.* Kate clung to that thought to give her a sense of security.

On the other hand, if her sister really were missing, of course she'd drop everything and hop on the first flight to Seattle. She felt uneasy just cancelling work and reorganizing her life on the whim of this woman she barely knew. Kate had photo shoots in the Los Angeles area lined up all week. People depended on her, so she wanted to be sure it was warranted.

"Kate. Your sister is missing! You really need to come as soon as possible," Suki pressed. "Surely, you don't have anything to do that's more important than this, do you?"

Kate recognized the guilt card being played. Her late mother had been a master at it.

"No, of course not. Nothing's more important than finding my sister, if she really *is* missing. However, I am going to call the police first and see what they say. You may be correct about the twenty-four hour thing, but I want to know for sure."

"Then you'll come?"

As much as Kate hated the thought of upending her whole world overnight, she had to seriously consider the possibility that Suki might be right. If Whitney needed her, she had no choice but to go to Seattle on the first flight she could get.

"Yes, yes, I'll come, but I am going to talk to the police as soon as we hang up. After that, I'll check for flights out of L.A. tomorrow." Kate would have to wait until the morning to change her work schedule, too. "I appreciate you letting me know, Suki. I'll be in touch."

~*~

Suki hung up from her conversation with Kate and immediately made another call.

"Hullo," a young man answered.

"It's done."

CHAPTER 2

"HEY, LADY! YOU'RE UP," a young male's voice came from behind her.

"What?" Startled, Kate looked around.

"You're up, over there at the counter." The impatient teenager pointed to the airline ticket counter.

His voice had jerked her out of a daze. She'd been standing in the long, slow-moving passenger line, replaying her situation and the unproductive conversation with the Seattle Police. She hadn't been able to get beyond talking to the officer at the front desk because Whitney had not been missing long enough. He hadn't told her anything of value one way or the other, except that if she was really concerned, she should come as soon as possible. Of course she was concerned. She loved her sister. How dare he suggest otherwise.

It was because of that bond, that if there was any chance Whitney actually *was* missing, Kate would drop everything and go. She had arranged to fly to Seattle on the next available flight.

Unfortunately, getting to Seattle was not so easy. Engine trouble on her connecting flight from Salt Lake City had forced the plane down in Boise, where she had to spend the night.

"Sorry," Kate muttered to the people in line behind her. Her face reddened and she rushed to the counter, slapping her driver's license down on the counter a little harder than she'd intended.

The ticket agent glared at her, then moved like a snail. Kate was sure she must have offended the woman. Glancing up at the monitor on the wall, it showed that her Horizon flight to Seattle was departing in twenty minutes.

Kate checked her watch for the umpteenth time, feeling her heart thumping in her chest. *Come on, come on, come on, lady! I have a plane to catch!* She tapped a staccato beat with the heel of her shoe.

Finally, the ticket agent offered up her pass. Kate grabbed it, tossed her long tresses over her shoulder and spun around to run for the security gate.

Splat!

Kate normally considered herself a controlled, refined, twenty-eight-year-old woman. But here she was, sprawled out face first on the hard floor, having tripped over a child's rolling backpack that she neglected to see in her haste. A manly, well-groomed hand reached down and helped her up. Mortified, her cheeks flushed a bright red.

The helpful hand belonged to an attractive man who looked to be in his early thirties. Kate could not help noticing his deep green eyes, thick brown hair and the broad shoulders filling out his fleece pullover.

"Are you okay?" His voice was warm and deep.

"Yes," she replied, her face flashing hot. "All, except my pride. Thanks for the help."

She scrambled to gather up her purse and coat and made a beeline for the security gate. Under any other circumstances, she might have been happy to linger and talk to the helpful stranger, but not today.

Finally, reaching the security gate, Kate flashed her boarding pass and driver's license at the beefy TSA official and took her place in line for the scanners. While waiting her turn, she noticed a young man in the next line over, putting his dull green backpack on the conveyor and stepping up to the scanner. He was about her age and wearing a navy blue baseball cap that covered his mop of curly brown hair. In the next moment, he and his backpack were pulled out of line and given the extra wand treatment.

"Oh, come on! Are you kidding me? I'm gonna miss my flight!" he complained, holding his arms straight out from his sides, while another TSA agent rummaged through his pack.

I can't afford to be singled out and delayed like that, she thought, trying not to stare. Efficiently loading her purse, shoes, and jacket in a gray plastic bin, she set it on the conveyor belt.

Checking her watch again, she was acutely aware that time was ticking down. If she could get through this security check without incident, she would have a good chance of making her flight. Kate handed her boarding pass to the female TSA worker on the other side of the full-body scanner, stood against the scanner as instructed, trying her best not to think of what the male TSA worker was looking at on the screen.

9

Thankful she was not detained, Kate scooped up her things, hurriedly stepped into her shoes and set off for Gate A-10. Following the overhead directional signs, she dashed down the wide corridor and found her gate.

The last few passengers in the boarding line were entering the door to the jet-way. Kate made it just in time.

Once on the plane, she found her assigned seat, on the aisle, and stowed her purse and coat. She leaned her head back against the headrest, closed her eyes, and let out a long sigh.

"I see you made your flight." A deep and familiar voice came from the aisle next to her.

Kate opened her eyes and turned to see who was talking to her. It was the man who had helped her off the floor at the ticket counter. He was storing his carry-on bag in the upper compartment over his seat.

"Yes, yes, I did." She was a little surprised to see him. He must have rushed for the plane, too. Then she realized he must have been right on her heels the whole mad dash to their gate.

"Are you okay? That was a nasty spill you took back at the ticket counter. Anything bruised?"

"Just my ego. I'm fine, really." A twinge of embarrassment heated her cheeks once more.

"My name's Ryan, by the way," he offered with a friendly smile, as he took his seat.

Kate smiled back and was about to respond with her name when the young man with the baseball cap and the dull green backpack walked down the aisle between them. She was glad the extra security had not made him miss his flight. Then she turned her attention back to her dashing rescuer.

"I'm Kate. I—" She was cut off in mid-sentence by the commanding voice of the captain, booming over the loudspeaker, welcoming all the passengers and thanking them for flying with Horizon.

"Kate, what do—" Now he was cut off by the flight attendant asking everyone to fasten their seatbelts and turn off their cell phones, after which she proceeded to give the safety measure instructions. Ryan and Kate glanced at each other and grinned.

She looked forward to talking with her new acquaintance a bit more on the flight, once the announcements were over. It would be a pleasant distraction from the crisis at hand, at least for a little while.

"Kate," Ryan said, once the flight attendant was finished, "are you from Boise?"

"No," she answered. "I live in Los Angeles. I'm a photographer there."

"Oh, I would have guessed a model, not the person behind the camera."

"Thank you, that's sweet," she said, "but no."

"Are you going to Seattle on business?"

"No." She was silent for a moment, floundering over a safe answer. "I'm going to see my sister. She lives there." Kate wasn't ready to tell this perfect stranger that her sister was missing, and she was going there to help find her. "Are *you* from Boise?"

"Yes...well, I was. I grew up here, went to Boise State. Then I moved to Seattle after graduation. You know, to make my fortune in the big city and all."

"What do you do?" Kate asked.

"I'm a real estate agent. Fortunately, the housing crash hasn't hurt the Seattle area as bad as it has in other parts of the country, so I do pretty well."

"Home for a visit?"

"Yeah. I came for the weekend to see my mom and dad and go to a Boise State football game with them. My mom and dad are diehard BSU Bronco fans. They love their blue turf."

"You can't be serious." Kate thought Ryan was kidding her.

"Even ESPN loves it. If you're ever watching college football on TV and the grass looks blue, you'll know it's Boise State."

She raised an eyebrow.

"So tell me, why are you in Boise?" he asked. "Weren't there any direct flights from Los Angeles?"

Kate told Ryan about the flight troubles that had landed her—literally—in Boise. "That's why I had the little mishap at the ticket counter—I was just so rushed. Thanks again for helping me up."

"I'm glad I could be of service, ma'am," Ryan said, as he pretended to tip his invisible hat. "Perhaps we could get a coffee or something while you're in Seattle."

"Maybe." She nodded, not knowing what she would find once she got to Seattle.

Kate appreciated the mental diversion for a while, but her sister was never far from her thoughts.

~*~

The piercing voice of one of the flight attendants blared over the loudspeaker telling everyone to make sure their seatbelts were fastened and their trays were put away, as they were preparing for their final descent into Seattle. *What lousy timing.* Ryan was just about to ask Kate for her phone number so they could meet for coffee, but the landing announcement cut him off.

He found Kate attractive and engaging and wanted to spend more time with her. Now that they had landed, the pent-up passengers all made a mad dash to retrieve their carry-ons from the overhead bins and jostled their way off the plane. Since Kate had no carry-ons, except her purse and jacket, she immediately joined the throng of passengers moving forward to get off the plane. Ryan had to wait for a clearing to get his bag out of the overhead and lost sight of her.

Disappointed, he headed for the baggage claim area. He would casually ask for her number while they stood around waiting for their bags to come up on the carousel.

However, when he reached the baggage claim area, she was nowhere to be found. He walked around the luggage carousel several times, he searched through the crowd, but she was not there. He had sensed a connection with this stunning woman, but now he had no way of contacting her.

When his suitcase finally came up on the carousel, he grabbed it and took the escalator down to the outdoor loading area. Peering up and down the roadway, he still hoped to catch a glimpse of her waiting for a cab or a shuttle, but she was not there either. Disheartened, he hailed the next taxi in line and went home.

CHAPTER 3

THE NOISY BAGGAGE CLAIM OFFICE had been packed with people from the troubled flight the night before, and the agent appeared overwhelmed with finding everyone's luggage. Anxious to get to Whitney's apartment to speak with her roommate, Kate was relieved to finally have her luggage. As she waved down the next taxi, she could have sworn that it was Ryan's silhouette in the backseat of the cab she saw speeding away.

The yellow car pulled up. Kate threw her bags in the trunk and she was off to her sister's apartment in the Belltown district of Seattle. In the smelly backseat of the well-worn cab, she sat in contemplative silence, mulling over questions she wanted to ask Suki.

Before she knew it, she had arrived. After paying the cab driver and retrieving her bags, she wheeled her luggage to the apartment building entrance.

A young man was leaning against the far left edge of the building, she noticed, smoking a cigarette. When she approached the building, he hurried away. He looked a lot like the disheveled young man with the ball cap and dull green backpack from her flight. *That was odd.* She shrugged off the uneasy feeling. There were more important things to deal with.

Kate pushed the intercom button by the entry door. Whitney's loft apartment was number 310.

"Yes?" a youthful female voice came over the scratchy speaker.

"This is Kate, Whitney's sister. Can you buzz me in?"

"Oh, yeah. Sure."

Kate heard the buzz and a click of the lock release. She pushed the door open and found an *Out of Order* sign on the elevator. She sighed. Just what she needed after a long night. She hauled her suitcases up the three flights of stairs, and then, out of breath, she knocked on the apartment door. Whitney's roommate opened it.

Suki had a head of deep red curls, layered to frame her round face. The red hair set off her sky-blue eyes. Dressed in a T-shirt and faded jeans, she looked like a teenager.

"Hi, I'm Kate."

"Yes, come in. I'm so glad you're here. I'm Suki," she said, extending her hand.

"Sorry I didn't make it last night. Like I told you on the phone, we had plane trouble," Kate replied, taking her hand.

"I'm glad you called and let me know about the delay. I've just been so worried about Whitney."

Kate pulled off her coat and draped it over her arm. There was something familiar about this young woman. "Have we met before?"

"No!" Suki cleared her throat. "I mean, no, I don't think so." She diverted her eyes and changed the subject. "Here, let me take your suitcase. I'll put it in Whitney's room for you." She dragged the heavy, wheeled bag down the short hallway and lifted it onto the partially made bed. Kate followed close behind with her smaller bag.

"Why don't you get settled and freshen up, and I'll make us some tea," Suki offered. "Then we can talk."

"That would be great. Thank you. I'll be just a few minutes." The creeping feeling of familiarity stayed with her.

Kate glanced around her sister's bedroom. The bedding was rumpled, a few tops thrown on the chair, shoes overflowing out of her closet. Whitney was not the meticulous person Kate was, but that was one of the things she loved about her sister. She was bubbly and carefree—a genuine free spirit. Kate wished she were more like Whitney in that way.

She walked into the open kitchen area to see Suki with a kettle of water that had just started to whistle. A plate of what appeared to be blueberry muffins was set out on the table. "Looks like I'm just in time," she said, trying to lighten the mood before digging into the serious business of her sister's whereabouts.

"Yes, you are. Just in time. Take a seat. There are muffins on the table if you're hungry. I have green tea and Chai tea. Which one would you like?"

"Green, please." Although it didn't really matter. Kate wished the girl would just sit down and stop fluttering about so they could talk.

Finally, Suki set the mugs down and sat.

Kate blew on the steaming tea, taking a moment to organize her thoughts.

"Suki, I have a lot of questions for you."

"I figured you would."

"Exactly when was the last time you saw my sister?"

"Well, it was the day before I called you. Saturday— like I told you on the phone. Yes, that was it, Saturday. Whitney had the day off, but I had to work. I left the apartment midmorning. She never mentioned anything about having any plans that evening, but when I got home and she wasn't here, I just assumed she had a date or went out with friends."

"Has Whitney ever stayed out all night before?" Kate asked.

"No, never. At least not since we've been roomies."

"Can you give me the names of any friends she might have gone out with?"

"Maybe a few. I'll write them down for you."

"What about a boyfriend?"

"No, I don't think there was anyone she's been dating recently."

"How about anyone at her office, someone she was having problems with?"

"She never mentioned it if she did."

"I know these are probably the same questions the police asked you when you filed the missing person report," said Kate.

"Police?" Suki asked.

"You *did* call the police and file a missing persons report, didn't you?"

"No. Like I told you on the phone, I think you have to wait twenty-four hours."

"That was Sunday night, Suki. It's been well over twenty-four hours. You didn't call them yesterday?"

This girl can't be that dumb, can she? Kate drew in a breath and centered herself.

"No, I was waiting for you," Suki replied, sounding defensive.

"Oh, Suki." Kate felt her eyes grow wide with panic. "Today is Tuesday. The police don't even know Whitney's missing. That means they're not even looking for her yet!" Her voice rose, despite her efforts to keep it level.

"But you told me when I first phoned you, that you were going to call the police yourself. So, I thought you had called them," Suki shot back.

"I did call them, but they wouldn't even talk to me because Whitney had just gone missing. I don't even think the officer wrote her name down. But that was Sunday night. Now it's Tuesday, Suki. Tuesday!"

Kate was frustrated with Suki's lack of urgency, and she didn't care to try to hide it. She shot up out of her chair. "We need to go down to the police station. Right now. Do you have a car?"

"Yes, but—" Suki began.

"But, nothing, Suki. We've got to get down to the police station and file the report."

"Okay, okay. You're right." She raised her hands in submission.

"Then, come on. Grab your car keys and let's go." Kate sprinted down the hall to the bedroom to get her purse and jacket.

~*~

After a stressful and silent drive, Suki and Kate arrived at the police station. They approached the reception desk where a middle-aged receptionist with graying brown hair stood looking bored.

"How can I help you?" she asked.

"I'd like to file a missing person report," Kate said.

"Let me get an officer for you." The receptionist picked up the phone.

Shortly, a big, burly man with a dark brown buzz cut approached the reception desk with a clipboard in his hand. Maybe now they could get to business.

"I'm Officer Delgado. What can I do for you ladies?"

"I'd like to file a missing person report," Kate stated.

"Who's missing?" he asked matter-of-factly, looking her in the eye.

"My sister, Whitney McAllister."

"How long has she been missing, ma'am?"

"Since Saturday, I believe."

"Saturday? Why have you waited so long to come in?" he asked.

"I was traveling, and we had a mix-up on who was calling you."

"Um, sorry, sir, I thought we had to wait. Guess I was wrong. So, can we just get it done now?" Suki looked sullen, and Kate fought down the urge to say something cutting.

"Sure. Here's the form," he muttered, as if he'd done it a thousand times before. He handed Kate a stack of forms on a brown pressed-wood clipboard with a pen attached by a string. "Go sit over there." He motioned to the chairs lined up against the wall. "Bring the form back to me when you're done, and I'll get a detective to talk to you."

"Thank you," Kate replied.

Suki just shrugged.

The young women each took a chair, and Suki helped Kate fill out the forms. When they were done, they handed the clipboard back to the officer.

"Wait here just a minute, ladies, and I'll get that detective." He disappeared through a doorway.

Kate looked at her watch, and then over at Suki, eager to get the process started. She figured her sister's roommate had first-hand knowledge of Whitney's activities—may have been the last person to see her—so she was glad to have Suki along. She just couldn't figure out why she hadn't filed the missing person report first thing Monday morning. It didn't make sense...unless there was something Suki wasn't telling her.

Suki stood abruptly. "I have to go to work. You can take it from here, can't you?"

"What?" Kate was taken aback.

She had assumed Suki would want to be there to help her, to talk with the police. "This is important. Can't you stay for a little while?"

"I can't be late for work again, and I've told you all I know." Suki started for the exit. "You can handle it from here."

"Wait." Kate called after her. "Please, don't go."

"I have to. Sorry."

Kate knew she couldn't make Suki stay. "All right. I'll do what I can without you. Maybe the detectives can call you later if they have questions. Okay?"

"Sure, sure," Suki agreed, backing toward the door.

"Wait! I need a key to get back into the apartment."

Suki twisted a key off the key ring as she walked back to Kate. She handed it to her. "I know where the spare key is hidden." She walked away.

It's okay, I can handle this. Kate took slow, deliberate breaths. *It's my sister who's missing—not Suki's. I can take a cab back to the apartment. Just breathe—*

"Miss McAllister?"

"Yes," Kate answered, sticking the key in her pocket as she turned around to her name being called.

"Hi, I'm Detective Raj Patel." He extended his hand. He was a man of average height, mid-thirties, sharply dressed in a dark gray suit with a black tie. "Why don't you follow me back to my desk, and I'll get a little more information from you. Right through this doorway," he said as he pointed toward the opening.

Kate followed him into the large, open squad room. There was a buzz of activity, with a handful of detectives in the room working on other cases, some on the phone, others typing away at their computers. The smell of stale coffee hung in the air. Patel led her to his desk.

She sat down across from him and relayed everything she knew, from what Suki had told her. "It's all there in the report," she said, pointing to the papers he held in his hand.

"That's not much to go on, Miss McAllister. But I assure you we'll do everything we can to try to find your sister."

Kate agreed that the information Suki had given her was sparse, but it just had to be enough. It had to. Whitney was all the family Kate had left. Trying not to panic, she focused again on Detective Patel.

"I'm kind of curious, though," he said. "If she's been missing since Saturday, why did you wait until today to report it?"

Kate told the detective the situation.

"I thought Suki would have come here yesterday to file the report, and I'm not really sure why she didn't. She gave me some lame excuse that she was waiting for me. I thought that was really odd."

"Yeah, it is," the detective agreed, writing a note on the form.

"Maybe she *was* waiting for me to do it—I don't know. I couldn't really get a straight answer out of her."

"It's a shame we've lost a whole day that we could have been working this case," Patel remarked.

"I know," Kate responded, clenching her teeth. "I was furious with Suki when she told me she hadn't filed a report yet. That's why I made her drive me down here right away."

"She didn't come in with you?" he asked.

"She did, for a little while. She helped me fill out the report. Then, all of a sudden, she claimed she had to leave to go to work."

"Sounds like you don't believe her."

"I don't really know her well enough to know for sure, but it just seemed out of the blue. Nothing makes sense." Kate worried her hands in her lap.

"I see. Hmmm. We'll definitely want to talk to her." He made another note on the report.

"If you let me borrow your pen, I can give you her number," Kate offered.

Kate jotted down Suki's phone number from the call records on her cell phone.

"Thanks, I'll give her a call," he said, looking at the pad. "Well, if you have nothing more, Miss McAllister, I think we're done here. We'll keep you posted."

Kate stood up, thanked him and shook his hand once more.

"Oh, wait. Before you go," Patel said, almost as an afterthought, "let me introduce you to Will Porter." Patel motioned to an African-American man to come over to them. Porter was tall and thin and looked to be about forty years old. He was standing across the room speaking with another detective. "He's my senior partner."

"Senior partner? Does that mean you're new at being a detective?" Kate asked Patel, her confidence in him waning a bit. *I need somebody who knows what they're doing.*

"Well, yes, but Detective Porter will be on this case with me. He's been doing this for about ten years, so between the two of us, we'll get the job done. Don't you worry."

How could she not worry? Her sister was missing. She bit down on her lips to keep those thoughts to herself.

"Miss McAllister, this is Detective Will Porter." As Patel introduced them, the senior detective reached out and shook hands with Kate, a serious look on his face.

"Will," Patel said, "Miss McAllister has just filed a missing person report for her sister. I told her we'll do everything we can to find her." Patel handed the file to Porter.

"Miss McAllister," Porter started, glancing over the forms she filled out.

"Call me Kate, please."

"Okay, Kate. Detective Patel and I will read over the report. We'll be in touch. Oh, and make sure we have your cell number so we can reach you."

"It's on the top form, there," she told him, pointing at the file. "I'd appreciate being kept in the loop."

"Certainly," Porter promised, opening the folder. "I don't see a photo of your sister in here."

"Oh, sorry, I forgot to ask about that," Patel apologized. Kate frowned at the critical oversight.

"We'll need one we can use to get the word out, Kate. We'll send it to our network of law enforcement agencies, the news media as well," Porter told her. "Do you have one with you?"

"Yes, I think I have a couple in my wallet," Kate replied, opening her bulky leather handbag and rummaging around inside. She pulled two different photos out of her wallet and handed them to Porter. He clipped them inside the file.

"Do you know if your sister has a computer or iPad or anything?" Porter asked.

Kate rolled her eyes up, searching her memory. "Oh, yes, I remember seeing a laptop in her bedroom."

"We'll need that. I always like to start with checking the subject's calendar and e-mails. Can we come with you right now and pick it up?" Porter asked.

"Oh, I'm sorry," Patel interrupted sheepishly, "I, uh, have a lunch appointment in a few minutes. I won't be long."

Porter frowned at him. "I'll take care of it."

"Let me walk out with you guys," Patel offered.

Once outside the station, Kate paused at the bottom of the front steps. She wanted to thank the detectives for their help, but before she could utter a word, she heard a man's voice calling her name.

She turned, to find out who it was, and was stunned to see it was the man from her flight.

"Kate, what a surprise!" Ryan's pleasure in seeing her was evident on his face.

"Ryan? What are you doing here?" Kate asked.

"You know each other?" Detective Patel questioned.

"Yes, we met on the plane from Boise this morning," she answered.

"Small world. Ryan is my lunch appointment," Patel said. "He's helping me buy a condo."

"It *is* a small world," Kate commented.

"I missed you at the baggage claim area...I wanted to get your phone number so we could have that coffee you promised me." He winked at her.

Kate pulled one of her business cards out of her purse and handed it to him.

Ryan's expression quickly changed, as if it had just dawned on him that she was coming out of the police station with a couple of detectives. "I'm sorry. I didn't mean to interrupt anything."

"You didn't," she replied.

"Is everything okay?" Ryan asked.

Kate looked at Patel, then at Porter, wondering how much she should divulge. She didn't find the answer in their faces, so she went ahead and told Ryan.

"Not really. My sister is missing. That's the real reason I came to Seattle."

"Oh, Kate. I had no idea. I thought you were just here to visit her."

"I wish—but no."

"If there's anything I can do to help, anything at all, just ask." Ryan pulled his business card out of his shirt pocket too and handed it to her. "My cell phone's on there."

"We've gotta go," Porter spoke up, tapping his wristwatch. "Time's a-wasting. I'll see you back here in about an hour, Raj. Take it easy, Ryan."

CHAPTER 4

BACK AT THE APARTMENT, Kate turned Suki's key in the door, letting herself and Detective Porter into the loft.

"Nice place," he said, glancing around the main living area and open kitchen of the small loft. "Where's the laptop?"

"It's in Whitney's bedroom. Wait here and I'll get it for you." She started off down the hallway.

"Do you mind if I take a look?" Porter asked. "Maybe I can see if there's anything that would give us a clue to where she went."

Kate stopped mid-way and spun around. "Sure, it's right this way."

Porter followed her down the short hallway and stepped in behind her. He stood still for a moment, surveying the room.

Queen-sized bed, neatly made, with a couple pieces of luggage on it, a chair with a coat thrown over it, a dresser with a plant and some framed photos—nothing out of place, as far as Kate could see.

"Have you moved anything since you arrived?" he asked.

"No. We just put the suitcases on the bed," she answered. "Well...that's not totally true. I did make the bed and put a few of her clothes and shoes away."

"Hmmm. Hopefully that won't matter," he said.

The open laptop sat on a small desk, a few sticky notes adhered to the desktop and a couple of pens next to it. Porter seemed to be reading one of the sticky notes. He frowned and tilted his head.

Kate wondered if that meant something.

"Who's Suki?"

"My sister's roommate," Kate replied. "Why?"

He pointed to one of the notes. On it was written 'Suki & guy (?)'. "I ask because your sister wrote her name on this sticky note with a question mark. It's probably nothing, but I'm going to take the note with me." He put on a thin latex glove, gently pulled the sticky note free and placed it in a small plastic evidence bag that he took from his jacket's breast pocket. After sliding the bag back into his pocket, he closed the laptop and picked it up.

"I hope you can find something—anything—in that computer that'll tell us where she is." Kate was desperate for any clue, no matter how small.

"I'll get one of our forensic techs on it as soon as I get back to the station. And if you think of anything else, let us know right away." The detective began to walk toward the door, and then he stopped and turned back to Kate.

"Do you know the roommate's full name?"

"Suki Gorman is all my sister ever told me."

"What can you tell me about her?" he asked.

"Not much. Whitney didn't talk about her very often, and I'd never met her until I arrived today. Why do you ask?"

"We just want to be thorough and cover all the bases. She was the last one that we know of to see Whitney—I'll run a background check on her, just to be safe."

Kate walked Detective Porter to the door and said good-bye as he walked out. She closed the door, and rested her back against it, wondering if Suki could have been somehow involved in Whitney's disappearance. It didn't seem likely, but at this point, she couldn't rule anyone out.

~*~

Suki worked the afternoon shift at Seattle's Underground Tour. It was a tourist attraction sitting about twenty feet below a portion of the current downtown area, known as Pioneer Square. The tour of the underground gives visitors a look at parts of the original city of Seattle.

Her final tour of the day was over, and she watched the last of her group go into the basement-level souvenir shop. She looked around to make sure no one was watching her, then ducked back into the tunnel and returned to the underground city.

Making her way through the web of corridors, she came to a locked door that she had blocked with an old diner's sign, a remnant from an historic café. The word *Dino's* in broken blue light bulbs outlined the marquee.

As a tour guide, Suki was familiar with all the tunnels and boarded-up areas not open to the public. However, a tour guide did not get a set of keys to the buildings and locked areas. So, in order to carry out her part of the scheme, she needed to get her hands on the keys. She and her brother, Ethan, had spent a long time setting up their revenge on Kate—those keys were an important step in that plan.

Thinking back on how she had had to flirt with surly old Gus, the forty-something head maintenance man, to get his keys, she felt a little sick to her stomach, but it had to be done. Once she had him sufficiently interested, she invited him to have drinks at the nearby Lucky Shamrock Tavern, a bar she knew he frequented. After snuggling with him in a booth and plying him with liquor, she actually found it rather easy to lift his set of keys.

She had heard through the grapevine that when Gus showed up for work the next day without them, and confessed he didn't know where they were, he was put on suspension. *Too bad for Gus*, Suki thought. He was nothing more than collateral damage to her.

She dragged the heavy, metal sign out of the way and unlocked the door. Pulling a small flashlight out of her jacket pocket, she switched it on and crept into the dark, hidden storage room.

The place ran about thirty feet deep and half as wide. Originally, it had been a shop of some sort in Seattle's early days. The room now held mostly old equipment and discarded boards. But back in the farthest rear corner, was an old metal twin bed covered with a thin, dirty mattress. A large rusty bucket sat beside it.

"Whitney?" Suki sang her name softly as she stroked her cold hand against her captive's cheek. The girl flinched from the icy touch, but it didn't seem to wake her. Suki gently shook Whitney's shoulder. Still she didn't rouse. She swept her flashlight over Whitney's body, and she shook her again.

"Whitney, wake up!" Suki said, forcing her voice through clenched teeth.

The woman on the bed stirred. Her hands and feet were bound with rope, which was then tied to the bed frame at both ends. A piece of duct tape covered her mouth. Her blue jeans and black sweater were rumpled, likely from writhing against her restraints. Her gray hooded sweatshirt was folded under her head into a makeshift pillow.

Suki yanked the tape off.

Whitney yelped. "Ouch!" She woke with a start and tried to sit up, seeming unaware that her hands and feet were tethered.

"Where am I?" Whitney questioned, struggling to pull an arm in front of her face to shield her eyes until they adjusted to the harsh and sudden light. Her short blonde hair was mussed, her mascara smudged. Whitney went limp against the mattress, trembling.

This was not the first day Suki had come to check on her and tend to her *needs*, yet the total darkness and drugs continued to cause the confusion that Suki had intended. "It doesn't matter," she answered.

"How long...have I...been...here?" Her words came slow and slurred, as if she was drunk. She appeared to be struggling to wake up.

"That doesn't matter either," Suki said.

"I don't understand. Why am I here?" Squinting, she once again tried to shade her eyes from the light, directing her gaze toward her captor. "And what is that awful smell?" Whitney grumbled.

"I'd say peanut butter," Suki replied, trying to redirect her attention, not wanting to give away where she was being held. Anyone who had been to the Underground Tour knew there was always a damp, musty smell in the underground city.

"I assumed you must be hungry, so I brought you another peanut butter sandwich. I can't have you dying on me."

"What? What do you mean?" Whitney asked, still straining to look up at the shadowy figure behind the flashlight. "Please? Tell me what's going on."

Suki needed to keep her sedated enough that everything would just be an undecipherable fog. She couldn't have Whitney saying anything to the police—if she survived, that is.

"Um, well...just don't worry about it. Everything's gonna be okay, and you'll be out of here before you know it."

Setting the flashlight down on the ground, she pulled the flattened sandwich out of her denim purse. She had again ground up several sleeping pills and mixed them into the peanut butter. It was easier to control Whitney if she was weak and sleepy. It was Ethan's idea, of course, but Suki had agreed.

She also brought a partial bottle of water so Whitney wouldn't get too dehydrated, but she wanted to minimize her fluids. She didn't want to have to help her to use the facilities very often to relieve herself, which was what the rusty bucket next to the bed was for.

"Let me help you sit up." She untied Whitney's hands from the bed but left them bound at the wrists. "You need to eat something."

Suki assisted Whitney to sit up as best she could, with her feet still tethered to the iron bed.

"I'm not hungry," Whitney slurred, barely able to keep her eyes open. "Why are you doing this to me?"

"Never mind." The less Whitney knew the better—for all concerned. "Now, eat this sandwich or I'm going to force you to." Suki shoved the sandwich toward her mouth. It had to be done. "Eat!"

Whitney's eyelids were heavy and even sitting up was an effort. Suki would make sure Whitney did not have the strength to fight, and she *would* eat the sandwich.

Suki tore off pieces and shoved them into Whitney's mouth, pouring water in after to make sure she swallowed.

Then, when the entire sandwich was gone, she applied a fresh piece of tape over her mouth and laid her back down on the filthy mattress, retying her hands to the frame.

"Now, go back to sleep, and it'll all be over soon," Suki promised as she walked away, leaving Whitney protesting weakly.

She opened the door slightly, peeking out and listening to see if anyone was out there. Not seeing or hearing anything, she quickly snuck out of the storage area. After securing the secret door, and dragging the Dino's sign in front of it once more, Suki slipped out through the busy souvenir shop and left unnoticed.

She drove home, wondering what happened with Kate and the police. Managing to find some street parking a couple of blocks away from her building, she walked home and took the elevator up to her apartment.

"About time they got that thing fixed," she mumbled under her breath, as she fumbled with the spare key.

~*~

Kate was on the phone, sitting at the dining table, her shoulders hunched and her hair pulled up into a large hair claw. "You didn't find anything at all on her computer?" Kate asked, her voice quivering.

She shook her head in disbelief. "I had hoped there'd be some clue, something in her calendar or in her e-mail, anything that would give us a place to start."

Kate sensed someone in the room and spun around to see Suki standing just inside the door, apparently eavesdropping on Kate's side of the conversation.

"Thanks for letting me know." Kate clicked her cell phone off and set it down hard on the table, next to her cup of tea. She looked at Suki as she walked in. "That was the police. They haven't found anything yet on Whitney's computer."

"Nothing?" She shrugged her coat off and hung it on the back of a chair. She didn't seem too concerned. "I'm sorry to hear that," Suki said, but her words sounded hollow and meaningless.

She put a patronizing hand on Kate's shoulder and patted it a couple of times. "It's going to be okay. They'll find her."

That seems rather gratuitous, Kate thought, shrugging off Suki's hand.

"Too much time is passing. What if they don't find her? What if she's—" Tears welled up in her eyes. Kate dabbed her tears with a napkin and took a shaky sip of her tea.

"They said they'd keep trying, didn't they?"

"Yes, but..." Kate replied weakly.

"Don't give up. I'm sure they'll come up with something." Suki turned and went to the stove to pour some tea for herself.

Kate stared after her, wondering if she detected a spring in her step. Just then, her cell phone rang. Startled, she pulled in a deep breath before answering it, expecting it to be the police again.

"Hello."

"Kate? This is Ryan."

"Ryan? Oh...hi," she said, sitting up straight in her chair, surprised to hear from him so soon. She had barely given him a second thought after running into him outside of the police station.

"I was thinking about you this afternoon," he told her. "Ah—I mean, because of your sister...you know?"

"I know."

"Has there been any word on her yet?"

"No, not yet, although we're not giving up," Kate said.

"Absolutely not. You've got to hang in there and keep that optimistic attitude."

"Thanks, it's just hard to sit here and try not to worry, waiting for a call from the police."

"I thought maybe I could help you out a little, Kate."

"Help me out? How?"

"Well, if you're not doing anything tonight, maybe you'd let me take you out to dinner, nothing fancy, just to take your mind off of things for a while."

"I don't know. I want to be available in case the police find anything."

"Raj, I mean, Detective Patel, has your cell phone number, doesn't he?"

"Yes."

"Then, he'll call you if they discover anything."

"Hmmm. I don't know," she said.

"You've got to eat, and I'll bet you could use a change of scenery."

"I guess you're right—I could use a break from sitting here fretting over things."

"I can be there in a few minutes if you're ready to go. What's your address?"

Kate gave him the address and thanked him for the invitation. Suki brought her cup of tea to the table while Kate was on the phone and leaned in, as if listening to her side of the conversation.

"See you soon," Kate said, clicking off the call.

"So, I guess you won't be here for dinner tonight?" Suki remarked, taking a seat. "I didn't know you knew anyone else in Seattle."

"Just Ryan. I met him on the plane from Boise." Kate removed the hair claw and shook her tresses out to fall free around her shoulders. "It turns out he's a friend of one of the detectives. Go figure." She rose from the table, and her slippered feet padded softly down the hallway to change her clothes for dinner.

Doubtful they would be going anywhere fancy, she pulled on a turquoise turtleneck sweater and off-white skinny jeans. Then, after freshening up her makeup and her hair, she checked her reflection in the mirror above the dresser.

She noticed a framed photo of herself with her sister, sitting on the dresser top. Kate picked it up and stared at it for a moment, running her finger over her sister's face. "You're all I have left." Struggling with the confusion of it all, Kate wiped at a rogue tear. "Where are you, Whitney?" she whispered sadly.

A sharp knock at the door caused Kate to jump.

"Ryan's here," Suki said, through the door.

"Already?"

"Yup."

"Tell him I'll be out in a minute." Kate took one last look at her sister's smiling face, carefully set the frame back down on the dresser, and inhaled deeply. Then she noticed Whitney's favorite perfume, Tatiana, sitting on the dresser among her jewelry box and other personal items. She spritzed a little on her sweater, to symbolically bring her sister closer to her. She breathed in the scent to fortify herself.

Picking up her black leather jacket, she went out to greet her new friend. "Hi, Ryan," Kate said, as she came into the living room. "I didn't expect you so soon."

Ryan was sitting on the sofa waiting, watching the evening news on the television. He stood as she entered, his deep green eyes lighting up and a broad smile spreading across his lips. "You look great."

"Thank you," she replied, giving him a grateful smile in return.

"Mmmm...you smell really good, too. What's that scent?"

"It's my sister's perfume, Tatiana. It's her favorite. So, I thought I'd try it."

"Well, it smells nice."

"Hey, look!" Kate pointed to the television. "They're talking about Whitney."

"Let me turn it up." Ryan picked up the remote control.

Kate stood still and stared at the screen, listening to the broadcaster give details of her missing sister. The photo that flashed across the screen had been taken earlier in the year when Whitney had come to L.A. for a visit. Tears rushed to the surface as memories of their happy time together flooded into her mind.

Ryan must have noticed her reaction to the story. "Are you doing okay?" He handed her a box of Kleenex that sat on the coffee table.

"Thanks," she said, pulling a tissue out. She dabbed under her eyes.

"Are you sure you're up to going out?"

Kate nodded her head. "I may not be great company tonight, but if you still want to have dinner with me…"

"I'm just here to help."

"And I appreciate it, really." Kate looked around for the roommate, but she had disappeared. "Suki," she called down the hallway, "we're leaving."

"Okay," the answer came from the direction of her bedroom.

Kate and Ryan had decided not to wait for the elevator, instead taking the stairs down the three flights. As they were descending the final flight, they passed a teenage girl and then, a few moments later, the familiar young man in the navy ball cap going up.

"Did you see that guy?" Kate asked after the man had passed, looking up the staircase. "The one with the baseball cap that was running up the stairs."

"I saw a young guy, maybe mid to late twenties, but I didn't really get a good look at him. Why?"

"I've seen him several times. First, at the Boise airport this morning, then he was on our flight, and then again outside this apartment building earlier today...," an uncomfortable chill ran up her spine, "...and now."

"Do you think he's following you?" Ryan asked, a hint of concern resonating in his voice.

"I don't know. It kind of gives me the creeps."

"Maybe you should mention it to Raj," he suggested as he held the heavy door open for her. "C'mon, the restaurant's this way." Ryan took a few steps in that direction.

"Where are we going?" Kate asked, putting on her jacket as she followed his lead. She expected they would be heading to his car.

"There's a great little seafood restaurant just down a couple of blocks, in one of the old brick buildings. Do you like salmon?"

"I love it."

"Then that's where we're going."

~*~

There was a rap on Suki's front door. She looked through the peephole. Her brother, Ethan, stood outside, appearing jittery and anxious, rocking from side to side. She opened the door and he ducked in.

"You should have waited longer to call. I think they saw me," he said, nervously, as he breezed past her. "They came down the stairs, Suki, not the elevator." He sounded irritated at her for not knowing the route they would take.

"Don't worry about it. Kate doesn't know who you are. Neither does her friend."

"I don't know about that. I mean, I don't think she saw me on the flight from L.A. to Salt Lake, 'cause I was sitting near the front of the plane and she was in the back, but I had to walk past her seat on the flight from Boise."

"I'm sure a lot of people walked past her seat, she probably didn't even notice you."

"But then, I was waiting outside your apartment building when she arrived this morning in a cab. I didn't expect to beat her here—somehow I did. I think I was able to walk away before she saw me, though."

"Ethan, you're going to have to be more careful, or she'll start suspecting something. She's pretty smart," Suki warned him.

"Well, if I would have been able to kill her in L.A., we wouldn't have had to drag her all the way up here."

"That was your own fault. You should have taken care of her there instead of involving me in your plan to lure her here." He had promised to leave her out of his obsession for revenge. Not only was he involving her, Whitney was now caught in the middle of it, as well.

"I couldn't get near her in L.A. She always had someone with her—friends, a boyfriend, her assistant. Her condo building has security, and whenever I tried to get her coming out of her condo, it seemed like there were cops constantly driving by."

"Excuses, excuses." Suki rolled her eyes and shook her head. "Did you have to take the same plane she was on?"

"My freakin' seat was way ahead of hers, and if we had come directly from L.A. to Seattle, like we were supposed to, she never would have seen me."

She glared at him. "You're just going to have to be careful and stay out of sight until it's show time."

"I will, Sis. I'm not stupid. I have this whole thing planned out." He shifted from foot to foot again, his arms gesturing wildly as he spoke. "Besides, she'll be dead before she figures it out."

"Why don't you sit down? You're making me nervous." Suki suspected he might be doing drugs again. He looked like he would need another hit soon.

"No, I'm good," he said, wiping his nose on his coat sleeve.

"Ethan," she grabbed his arm. "Are you on something? You look like you're tweakin'."

"I'm fine. Really, I'm fine," he answered, yanking his arm free and sticking his hands in his jacket pockets. "By the way, where'd you end up stashing that sister?"

"She's in a hidden storage area in the underground city, where I work...like we talked about. Don't you remember?"

"Uh, yeah, yeah, that's right, I remember now."

"No one will think to look for her there. I have her sedated, but I don't know how long I can keep her down there. I checked on her today after work. I'll go again sometime tomorrow."

"Don't worry about it. If she dies, no one will discover her for months, maybe even years," he said coldly.

"Ethan. It's not Whitney you're after. It's Kate. Whitney shouldn't have to die."

"Does it really matter? C'mon, Sis, I mean really."

"It does to me. I'm not a murderer," Suki declared.

"Oh, but you don't mind me killing Kate?" Ethan responded sarcastically.

"That's different. She deserves it. An eye for an eye, you know."

"Well, it doesn't matter to me. Besides, it'll all be over tomorrow." Ethan looked into the kitchen. "Hey, you got anything to eat in this place. I'm hungry."
"Sit down and I'll make us some sandwiches. Kate'll be gone for a while."

CHAPTER 5

RYAN AND KATE REACHED the restaurant just as a light rain began to fall. He pulled the heavy wooden door open for her, and they scooted inside, out of the drizzle.

"Welcome to Yellowfin's Seafood Grille. Table for two?" asked the twenty-something Asian hostess.

"Yes," Ryan replied.

"Would you like a booth?" she asked. There was a small Tuesday night crowd, so she was able to seat them right away.

"Sure, a booth would be great." Kate's gaze wandered around the restaurant as the hostess showed them to their booth along the front window. Her photographer's eye took in the beauty of the architecture and interior design. She admired the contemporary upscale décor—high ceilings, straight lines, a natural color scheme of greens and browns, a mix of steel and wood. A high wall of exposed brownish-red brick added to the ambience.

There was a casual elegance about this place that appealed to her. Ryan seemed to fit right in, with his black cashmere sweater, leather jacket and well-fitting jeans. "This place looks great, Ryan. I'm loving the décor."

She pulled her jacket off and laid it on the seat next to her.

"Me, too, it has a good vibe. Very *Pacific-Northwest-goes-upscale* kind of thing, don't you think?"

"I do." Kate nodded.

They read over the menu for a few minutes, which offered gourmet seafood entrees, and placed their orders when their waiter arrived.

"I'd like to hear which wine you suggest with the salmon?" Ryan asked.

"A bottle of white wine, a Chardonnay or a dry Riesling," the waiter replied.

"That sounds good," Kate agreed. "Chardonnay."

"Yes, it does. Let's have a bottle of your Chardonnay," Ryan ordered.

"Very good, sir, I'll have your dinners out shortly and be right back with the wine." He turned sharply and was gone.

"Thank you for inviting me to dinner, Ryan," Kate began. "I don't know what kind of company I'll be tonight, though. I keep wondering what could have happened to my sister and if she's all right. But I did really need to get out of that apartment. I've just been sitting, then pacing, sitting, then pacing, imagining the worst, waiting for news from the detectives."

"Happy I could help. Is Suki not good company?" Ryan leaned forward, folding his arms on the table and giving her his full attention.

"It's not that. Well, yes, she is a little odd, I have to admit. And I am still irritated at the time we lost by her not notifying the police, but that's not it." She lowered her eyes for a moment and tucked her hair behind her ear on one side, fingering her silver hoop earring.

"What is it, then?"

"It's just being in Whitney's place, you know?" Kate continued, raising her eyes. "Staying in her room, it reminds me every second that she's missing and something terrible might have happened to her. She's all the family I've got." As Kate met Ryan's eyes, she sensed he understood.

"Your wine, sir." The server reappeared, as if out of thin air. "Shall I pour?"

"No, I can do that," Ryan replied. "Thank you."

He set the bottle on the table and was off again.

"Tell me about your sister."

"Well, she's twenty-four, cute and outgoing, smart and creative. Blonde hair, blue eyes, like me."

"Long hair like yours?"

"No, she wears it short and kind of spiky."

"What does she do for a living?" he asked.

"She's an administrative assistant at Amazon's corporate offices. She got her degree in marketing from the University of Washington last year, so she's hoping to move up the ranks when there's an opening."

"What about your parents?" Ryan asked, pouring a little wine into both of their goblets.

"They both died in an auto accident a couple of years ago."

"I'm sorry to hear that. I can't even imagine how terrible that must have been."

"It took me quite awhile to get over it. I mean, who ever totally gets over something like that? But it's not as difficult talking about it now."

"And you have no other brothers or sisters?"

"No, just Whitney," she said, with sadness in her voice. She picked up her wine glass and took a small sip.

"Hmmm. Not even grandparents?"

"No, nothing. Our parents were in their forties when they got married and had us. All our grandparents have long since died. Mom had a sister who died as a child from pneumonia, and Dad was an only child. There may be some distant relatives back east somewhere, but we never knew any of them. Our parents moved out here to Seattle right after they were married. Dad went to work for Boeing."

"I thought you said you were from Los Angeles."

"No, that's where I live now," Kate explained. "I grew up here, in Seattle."

"Really? What part of Seattle?"

"Near Queen Anne Hill," she replied. "It's a beautiful area, but I don't need to tell you that. As a Realtor, you must know all the areas pretty well."

"Yeah, but I have to say Queen Anne Hill is my favorite, with its big handsome old homes. I'd love to buy a house there someday."

Kate remembered how her family would park there on weekends and walk along the sidewalks—Dad and Mom in the lead, commenting on gardens and the view, while she and Whitney trailed behind, more absorbed with teasing each other. "I haven't been up there in a long time."

"Why not?" Ryan asked.

"Because I went away to college in California. I came back here for a while, but after my folks died, I decided to move back to California."

"And here I thought you grew up in Los Angeles."

She took another sip of her wine. "And you said on the plane you were from Boise, right?"

"Yes, I grew up there. My parents still live on the outer edge of Boise, in the little town of Eagle. I try to go home to see them every few months."

"You're a good son."

"I am, aren't I," he chuckled and caught her gaze. Their eyes locked for a moment, until they were interrupted by the waiter setting their plates down.

Kate put her white linen napkin on her lap. She leaned her head slightly over her plate and breathed in. "It smells delicious."

The server nodded and was off to another table.

"Let's eat, I'm starved," Ryan said.

They both dug into their salmon and truffle risotto, savoring every bite. Ryan had been able to successfully take Kate's mind off of Whitney for at least a little while, and give her some reprieve from her worry. She was grateful for that.

"So, do you have any brothers or sisters?" Kate asked, as she finished off the last bit of her salmon.

"No. Well, I did," he answered. She could see a shadow of sadness fall over his face.

"What do you mean?" Kate was almost sorry she had asked. The words just slipped out before she could stop them. She sensed it was not going to be a pleasant story.

"I had a little sister. She was hit by a truck while she was out jogging one day. She was nineteen. It was early one winter morning, and a teenage boy hadn't cleared all the frost off his windows. He was driving to school and didn't see her until it was too late. She died that night."

"Oh, Ryan, I'm so sorry."

"It was a long time ago, nine years," he said. "She would have been twenty-eight now." He took a hard swallow from his wine glass. "I've gotten used to her not being around, but I still miss her when I think of her."

"I feel so bad that I brought it up," Kate said.

"It is what it is."

"So, you understand how important a sister is," she told him, looking into his kind eyes.

He held her gaze for a moment. "I do."

Their waiter returned and slipped the small bill folder onto the table, then refilled their water glasses. Ryan stuck his credit card into the black leather folder and handed it back.

Ryan smiled at Kate. Then, just as he was about to open his mouth to say something, they were interrupted once more.

A stunning dark-haired beauty with a deep and sultry voice slinked up to the table. "Hey, Ryan, I didn't know you were going to be here tonight."

"Oh, hi." Ryan seemed caught off guard and looked a bit uncomfortable.

The woman rested a hand on Ryan's shoulder and pulled her long raven hair to one side with the other, as she turned to look at Kate.

"Aren't you going to introduce us?" the woman asked, glaring at Kate.

Kate was taken aback, also. She raised her eyebrows and shot Ryan an impish grin before looking up into the face of the lovely brunette.

Ryan looked surprised.

Girlfriend or ex-girlfriend? Kate wondered. *He couldn't have known she'd be here, or surely he would have chosen another restaurant.*

He gritted his teeth and made the introductions. "Kate, this is Vanessa. Vanessa, this is my friend, Kate."

"Hello, Kate," Vanessa said, seeming to studying Kate's face and body language, as if she was assessing her competition.

"Hello," Kate returned.

"Have you two been dating long?" Vanessa inquired pointedly, a hint of jealousy in her voice. Vanessa was a little too direct for Kate's liking, she wondered if her expression gave it away.

"We're not dating. Kate's a friend. She's just in town for a few days," Ryan answered, apparently trying to dodge any more questions and perhaps to keep Kate's real situation a secret.

"That's right," Kate agreed, picking up on his attempt to shield her. "Ryan was kind enough to invite me to dinner so I didn't have to eat alone tonight. He's very thoughtful that way."

"Yes, he is." Vanessa's hand was still resting possessively on Ryan's shoulder. "Well, I just wanted to come over and say hello. I'd better get back to my table. We're here celebrating one of my friends' birthday. It was nice to meet you, Kate."

"Nice meeting you, too," Kate replied.

"And Ryan," Vanessa seductively leaned down and whispered in his ear, but loud enough that Kate could overhear, "don't be a stranger." Then she stood up straight, adjusted the short skirt of her tight-fitting dress and sashayed back to her party's table, as if she thought Ryan might be watching.

"Wow, who was that?" Kate asked, her eyebrows arching.

"An old girlfriend."

"You broke up with her, I'm guessing."

"What makes you say that?"

"Are you kidding?" Kate laughed. "Everything about her screamed. *Ryan, take me back!* Her voice, her body language. Oh, my gosh."

Just then, the waiter brought back Ryan's card.

Ryan continued, "Well, you're right. I broke it off with her, but she keeps trying to suck me back in. I've known her a long time. We met in high school and dated for a while back then."

"In Boise?"

"Yep."

"You were the football star and she was a cheerleader?"

"Something like that. After high school, I stayed in town and went to Boise State University. Vanessa came here to the University of Washington, and she ended up taking a job and staying. After I graduated, I moved here to work. It wasn't until I'd been in Seattle for a few years that we ran into each other one day at a Starbucks not far from here."

"That's when you started dating again?" Kate guessed.

"Not right away, but eventually, yeah. We dated for a few months, but after awhile I knew it wasn't going to work. We weren't the same people we were back in high school. Well, I wasn't the same anyway. She hadn't changed much. She was always pretty high maintenance, even back then. I thought she would have outgrown it by then, but no—it was starting to wear on me."

Kate had just observed Vanessa in action. It was easy for her to see that woman might be a handful for any man.

"After awhile it became clear our lives were going in two different directions. I wanted to settle down and have kids, she didn't. She wanted her career."

"There's nothing wrong with a career. I have a career," Kate pointed out, sounding a little defensive.

"I understand, but is that all you want? Don't you ever want a family?"

"Yes, I want a family, in time, but right now I want my career. I'm good at what I do and I love it."

"But a career can't love you back."

"True, but I figure with my photography business doing well, and working for myself, one day I can have both."

"Well, Vanessa is a paralegal, and she's thinking about going back to school to become a lawyer. She wants a husband, but having kids doesn't fit into her life plan."

"High maintenance or not, it sounds like kids are really important to you," Kate said.

"They are, and I made that clear to her, but she won't leave me alone. She thinks I'll change my mind about the children. I won't. That's why I—" Ryan paused as if deciding if he would finish the thought.

"That's why you, what?"

"When I walked away, I said I'd never look back, and—"

"When you walked away from Vanessa?"

"No. When I walked away from the force." Ryan looked at Kate as if waiting for a barrage of questions.

"You were a cop?" she asked, completely surprised by the revelation. "Wow, I had no idea. I can see it in you, though."

"Being a cop and having a family don't have a reputation for going hand in hand. I decided to get out before I became a weekend dad with two-point-three ex-wives and a high rate of suicide."

"It sounds like you know what you want."

"And right now I want to stop talking about Vanessa and get out of here." He smiled at her.

"Before dessert?" Kate teased. Her sweet tooth was showing.

"I *really* would like to get out of here," he repeated.

Kate could see Ryan was squirming.

"But, if you honestly want dessert...I'll take you to my favorite frozen yogurt shop down by the wharf. How does that sound?"

"Well, I *was* teasing, but sure, it sounds like a win-win. Relief from Vanessa for you and dessert for me." Kate smiled to herself as she pulled on her jacket and grabbed her purse. "Let's go."

Ryan stood up and took Kate's hand to help her slide out of the booth.

Kate noticed Vanessa watching them as they got up from their table. The angry look on her face exposed her feelings—she clearly thought that Ryan and Kate were more than just friends. And she didn't seem to like that idea.

CHAPTER 6

SITTING AT A LITTLE ROUND TABLE in Spoon Me, Ryan and Kate relished their cups of frozen yogurt—creamy chocolate covered with chopped-up Snickers bars. They soon discovered they both had an untamed sweet tooth, and chocolate was their decadence of choice.

"I was thinking, Kate," Ryan said, as he was about to devour the last spoonful of the frozen dessert, "it's still early. How would you like to drive up to Queen Anne Hill and take in the incredible views we talked about?"

She looked at the time on her watch, which read nine-forty-five.

"I wonder why we haven't heard anything from the detectives tonight." Although Ryan was a nice diversion from her worries for a couple of hours, Kate felt a little guilty for enjoying herself when her sister was missing.

"They probably don't have anything to tell you yet. If it would make you feel better, why don't you give them a call," he suggested.

She pulled out her phone and started to dial the number.

"Although," Ryan interjected, "it's almost ten o'clock. Unless there was a break in the case, they're likely at home by now."

"You're right. If they had anything to tell me, they would have called." She sighed, resigned to waiting to hear from them. She cancelled the dial and stuck the phone back in her pocket.

They left the yogurt shop and drove up toward Kerry Park in the Queen Anne Hill district. Before reaching the park, Ryan pulled his vehicle over and stopped in front of a charming blue-gray two-story home with white shutters. It had a *for-sale* sign planted in the front yard.

"Why are we stopping?" Kate asked.

"I just wanted to show you something. See that house right there, the one with the for-sale sign?"

"Yes, it's beautiful. Whose house is it?"

"It's a foreclosure, so it belongs to the bank now. I was toying with the idea of buying it, if I can negotiate a fantastic deal on it. It's the kind of home I'd like to raise a family in someday."

"It's very *Leave It to Beaver*."

"Is that a good thing?" he asked.

"Yes, I'd say so. What's it like inside?"

"Well cared for, big rooms, lots of woodwork. I previewed it last week. I'd show it to you now except there's no electricity on."

"Oh, too bad. Maybe tomorrow, if you have time." She didn't expect him to spend his time entertaining her, but unless something broke in the case, she would have a lot of hours on her hands. She'd like to fill at least some of them with something other than worry.

"Sure."

"Well, let's go see that gorgeous view you promised me."

Ryan drove her over to Kerry Park, a small crescent-shaped park built in tiers into the side of the hill, just a couple of blocks away. He pulled his Land Rover to the curb along West Highland Drive and hurried around to open Kate's door before she did. She wasn't used to such chivalry.

"You didn't need to open my door," she said. "I'm fully capable—"

"I know," he cut her off, "I didn't *need* to, but my mama taught me right."

She grinned at his colloquialism. They strolled across the sliver of a park, toward the metal railing, as the breathtaking skyline panorama opened up before them.

"Wow, Ryan. I'd forgotten how fabulous the city lights are from here." A beaming smile spread across her face.

"It is pretty spectacular," he agreed.

"Oh, and what a great view of the Space Needle," she exclaimed, unable to hold back her delight. "I remember how Mom and Dad used to like coming here. Mom told me sometimes they'd just sit on one of the benches and take in the stars and the city lights, and talk about their future."

Kate noticed Ryan watching her as she spoke about her parents. She wondered what he saw in her face. The excitement of a child? Sadness? Joy? Maybe all of that. He fidgeted as if he wasn't sure what he should do. He changed the subject, drawing her attention back to the beautiful view.

"Do you see that tall building with the rounded top, just to the left of the Space Needle?" he asked, pointing toward the building.

"Yes."

"That's where my office is."

"You must have a great view of the city."

"There's a view from some of the offices, unfortunately, not from mine. But it's okay, I get to see it often enough."

"Well, I don't. Thanks for bringing me up here, Ryan. It's breathtaking."

"And to think you traded all this for Los Angeles," he teased, making a wide sweeping motion with his hand, shaking his head. The gesture made her giggle.

"I have one of my cameras with me. I think I'll take a few shots so I can capture this and take it home with me." Pulling a small digital camera out of her purse, she adjusted a few settings and clicked an array of shots of the skyline.

Kate immersed herself in snapping photos, one of the few things that gave her pleasure these days. She felt Ryan's gaze on her.

She stuck her camera in her bag and turned to him. "I can't wait to get home and see these shots on my thirty-two-inch computer monitor. I'll have to show them to my friends back in L.A."

"Speaking of your friends in L.A., and I hope this isn't too personal, Kate, but do you have anyone special waiting for you back there?"

"Like a boyfriend?" she asked.

"Boyfriend, fiancé, significant other?" he asked wearing a hopeful expression.

"No, not at the moment."

"But there was someone?" he pried, seeming to sense there was more to the story.

"There was."

"Don't leave me hanging, Kate."

She wrapped her arms tight over her chest and turned back to the city view. "I don't really want to talk about it right now."

"You're right. It's none of my business. Sorry I asked."

"No need to be sorry. Maybe I'll tell you sometime. This evening has just been so lovely that I don't want to ruin it."

"It has been, hasn't it?" Ryan agreed. He draped his arm loosely around her shoulder and she leaned into him. They stood at the railing for a few minutes just gazing silently at the dazzling city lights.

The rain began to fall once more, suggesting it was time to leave.

~*~

Ryan was sitting at the computer in his office when he heard a voice outside his door.

"Knock, knock." The door eased open.

He looked up with a smile that quickly disappeared when he saw that it was Vanessa. He would have preferred it was Kate's face he saw.

Vanessa's own smile dropped, as she seemed to read the disappointment in his face. "Hello, Ryan. Are you busy?"

"Just working on the paperwork to get Raj Patel's condo purchase finalized and closed so..."

"Raj Patel? I haven't seen him in eons. How is he doing?"

"He's fine. What do you need, Vanessa?"

"I just thought I'd stop by and say hi. It was so nice running into you last night."

Ryan looked back at his computer screen and began typing again, hoping she would get the hint that he didn't want to talk to her. "Yeah, it was nice of you to come over to the table."

"I was wondering, if you're not doing anything this evening, maybe you'd like to come by my place for dinner. I have a new recipe for scaloppini I'm dying to try out. What do you say?" She batted her eyes in typical Vanessa fashion.

"I don't think so." He stopped typing and looked up from his computer to face her. "I don't see the point."

"Just a friendly dinner, Ryan."

He could see she was working to keep her voice light and casual, likely hoping he could not see through her ploy, but she couldn't help her voice rising. It was clear she was trying to reel him back in, but he was not having any of it. "No, I have other plans tonight. Sorry."

"You're not sorry at all!" she shrieked.

"Whoa, calm down."

"It's that blonde, isn't it?" Vanessa accused.

"I told you, we're just friends. I only met her yesterday morning on the plane from Boise." He didn't really want to go into too much detail with her, but he was trying to calm her down.

"You went home to Boise?"

"Yes, I flew home to see my folks over the weekend and was flying back. She sat across the aisle from me on the flight, and we had a little conversation." Not that it was any of her business, but maybe explaining things would get her out of his office faster.

"I don't believe you," she said, planting her hands on her hips.

"That's up to you." He flipped through a file on his desk, then stuck it in a drawer.

"There's more to it than that, Ryan. I know there is."

Irritated, he stopped shuffling the papers on his desk and looked her in the eye. "Okay, I'll bite. What do you know, Vanessa?"

She leaned forward and placed both hands on his desk. "I saw the way you were looking at her, and the way she was looking at you. There was definitely something going on between the two of you." She waggled her finger in his face to make her point.

"You were watching us?" Ryan stood up from his desk, his eyebrows knitting together.

She pulled upright, too, crossing her arms defensively. "I wouldn't say I was watching you, more like I happened to notice you a few times."

He saw she was back peddling now. She knew she couldn't insert herself back into Ryan's life if she made him mad. He wanted to grin, but thought better of it. "It's really none of your business."

"What's none of my business?" Vanessa pressed.

"Me and Kate."

"Aha! I knew there was something going on between you two."

"You're not going to quit, are you?" He sat back down in his chair.

"Quitting is not part of my DNA."

"All right, all right." Ryan raised his hands in surrender. "I'll tell you the truth so you'll drop it. Kate is only in town for a little while. I didn't want to tell you this last night, not in front of her, but—"

"But what?" she interrupted.

"She came to Seattle because her sister has gone missing. You may have heard about her disappearance on the news—Whitney McAllister?"

"That sounds familiar." Vanessa raised her eyes toward the ceiling, as if she was trying to remember something. "Wait! You said you met her on a flight from Boise?"

"Yes, so?"

"A story I read about a dead blonde woman...she was found in Boise."

"And?" He tried patiently to humor her, but his patience was running out.

"Maybe Kate killed her sister and dropped the body on the banks of the river," Vanessa exclaimed, as if she'd just solved a big mystery.

"That's enough, Vanessa! She didn't kill her sister. The fact that the woman is blonde is purely coincidental. Kate is here, working with the police as much as she can, trying to help find Whitney, but mostly she's just waiting for news from them."

"You sure jumped to her defense fast enough, didn't you?"

"I'm simply trying to be a friend." Ryan turned back to his computer.

"If you say so," she said, pursing her lips. "I'd better let you get back to work. Call me sometime, Ryan, won't you? I miss seeing you."

He nonchalantly waived a hand in the air.

"You know," she said as she opened his door and spun back toward him, "it could be her sister. Even if Kate didn't do it, someone could have kidnapped her and taken her out of state. You hear about it in the news all the time."

He raised his arm and pointed to the door without looking up from his work.

"I'm just saying...someone should tell the police to look into it." She sauntered out of his office, letting the door slam behind her.

CHAPTER 7

KATE HAD ENJOYED SPENDING TIME with Ryan and had been grateful for the distraction. However, once she'd gotten home and was lying in Whitney's bed, smelling her sister's perfume in the room, she had a hard time going to sleep. She'd tossed and turned most of the night, finally dozing off in the wee hours of the morning.

It was about ten o'clock the next morning when she'd dragged herself out of bed and into the bathroom to throw cold water on her face. Now, Kate sleepily wandered barefoot into the kitchen in her pink camisole and pajama bottoms to see if there was any coffee.

"Good morning, Kate." Suki greeted her cheerfully from a seat at the table, looking like she had already been up for hours. "You were out late."

"Not too late, but you must have already gone to bed." Kate stood by the table.

"Yeah, I'm not a night person. I like to get up early."

"It was only about eleven or so when I got home. I just couldn't sleep once I got into bed." Kate glanced around the kitchen. "I could really use some coffee."

"Why don't you sit down and I'll get you a cup," Suki offered. "The sugar and creamer are on the table." Suki poured the coffee and set it down in front of Kate. "How was your date?"

"Oh, it wasn't a date, it was just dinner," she replied, looking off in the distance, a little smile curling on her lips.

Kate set her cell phone down on the table, tore open a yellow Splenda packet and stirred it into her cup of coffee.

"Spill," Suki said, apparently interested in the details. "You were out pretty late for it to be just dinner."

Kate took a sip from her cup, and then set it down. "Well, there's nothing to tell, really. We went to a nice restaurant just down the street, Yellowfin's Seafood Grille."

"I've heard good things about that place."

"After dinner, we went and had frozen yogurt down by the water. Then, Ryan drove me up to Kerry Park to see the view of the Space Needle and the city lights." Kate took another a sip of her coffee. She noticed Suki flinch a little when she mentioned the view, but she couldn't imagine why.

Kate suddenly recalled something else, running into Ryan's old girlfriend. She was about to share the tidbit, but she decided to keep that to herself. The uneasiness she felt around Suki warned her that she'd better not disclose any more than necessary with the girl.

"By the way," Suki said, breaking into Kate's thoughts, "I have to go to work today, and I was wondering if you'd like to meet me down at the Underground Tours later. I'll show you around, it's pretty interesting. And it's definitely better than hanging out here all day waiting for the police to call you."

"I've always wondered what it was like down there in the creepy underground. Funny, I grew up here, but I've never been. What time should I come?"

"My first tour starts about noon. Why don't you meet me in the souvenir shop downstairs at eleven-thirty, and I'll give you a private tour before the others begin?"

"Sounds good," Kate replied.

"Hey, did you hear anything yet from the police?" Suki asked.

"No, nothing last night. I was hoping they would call this morning."

No sooner did the words come out of Kate's mouth than her cell phone began to ring. She picked it up from the table and saw it was Detective Patel calling.

"Hello, this is Kate."

"Kate, this is Detective Patel. We received a call a few minutes ago from the Boise Police Department. They found a young woman's body near the river that runs through their downtown. The woman matches Whitney's description."

"What?" Kate asked, her eyes widening, looking fearfully across the table at Suki. "Oh, God, please don't let it be Whitney," she muttered under her breath.

"Yes, a dead body and—" Patel started to say.

"Wait. The *Boise* Police Department?" Kate wondered if she had heard him correctly.

"Yes, Boise. Could Whitney have possibly gone to Boise for any reason?" he questioned.

"Not that I know of," she answered, her voice quivering, "but let me ask Suki. She's right here." Kate turned her attention to Suki. "Do you know of any reason my sister may have gone to Boise?"

"Boise? No. What would she be doing there?" Suki looked confused as to why Kate was asking.

Kate returned her attention to the phone. "Sorry, Detective, Suki says she doesn't know why Whitney would be in Boise, and honestly, I can't think of any possible reason either, unless..." Kate went silent and her bottom lip began to tremble.

"Unless what?" Patel asked.

"Unless someone kidnapped her and took her there against her will." Kate's voice cracked as she could barely get the words out.

"Unfortunately, that's what I was thinking, too."

Tears filled Kate's eyes. "Oh, God," she sighed.

"Let's not get ahead of ourselves, Kate. It's very likely that it's not even her. So let's slow down and take it a step at a time."

"You're right, but I don't understand why they would think that woman might be my sister?"

"Well, the police got a tip this morning. A lady called saying she saw a young woman that looked a lot like Whitney in the park near the river a couple of days ago."

"Who said that? Wait...how would someone in Boise know what Whitney looked like?" Kate asked.

"Anonymous caller, and I'm assuming from the television or the Internet. The caller must have seen a news

70

report and remembered seeing someone that looked a lot like the pictures," Patel explained.

"I hope that person was wrong," Kate replied, shaking her head.

"So do I, but we need to know, one way or the other. The Boise Police would like you to come down there and take a look at the body. You know, see if it's your sister. Can you do that as soon as possible, like today?"

"Yes, yes, of course. I'll get the first flight out of here."

"Okay then, I'll call them back and let them know you're on your way."

Kate hung up her phone, held it to her chest, and tears began running down her cheeks.

"What is it? What's wrong?" Suki asked, handing her a napkin.

Kate filled Suki in on what Patel had said. She took a deep breath, trying to stifle her tears. "They want me to come down there right away to see if it's Whitney or not."

"I'm so sorry, Kate," said Suki, patting her shoulder, suddenly seeming overly caring, based on her lack of participation in the search for Whitney.

"Thank you, but there's no need to be sorry yet. Let's hope it's not Whitney."

Suki just nodded.

Kate looked at the time on her phone. "I'd better call the airlines and see when the next flight is. I'm sure Horizon or Southwest must have several more flights going to Boise today." Kate scurried down the hall to the bedroom and closed her door.

She sat on the edge of the bed, and decided to phone Ryan before calling the airlines. If she had to go and identify her sister's dead body, she wanted someone with her for emotional support. She had not known Ryan very long, but she didn't have anyone else to ask. It was too long a trip for any of her L.A. friends, and there was no way she would ask Suki. That girl made her uneasy. There was something oddly familiar about her, but Kate just could not put her finger on it.

Recalling Ryan's number recorded in her phone, she punched the call button.

"Hello, this is Ryan Wilson, Keller Williams Realty. How can I help you?"

"Ryan, this is Kate."

"Kate! What a nice surprise."

"I need your help," Kate said.

"You sound serious. What is it?"

"I have to fly to Boise as soon as possible, and I'd like you to come with me, if you can."

"Boise? Why? What's going on?"

"Detective Patel just called me and said the Boise Police contacted him this morning. They have a body they want me to identify." Her throat tightened and her voice began to crack. She swallowed hard to relax her throat and regain her composure. "They think it might be my sister."

"Oh, Kate. I'm so sorry. I don't even know what to say."

"Say yes," she pleaded. "Say you'll come with me. I don't want to do this by myself."

"Okay. Yes, I'll come with you. I'll just need to change a few things around."

"I'm sorry, I don't mean to be a bother. You probably have clients to see today."

"No bother. I'll just have my assistant reschedule a couple of appointments for me, nothing earth shattering," he said, looking over his calendar, "and then I'm out of here. When is the flight?"

"I haven't called the airlines yet. I wanted to talk to you first, to see how many tickets I needed to get."

"Don't worry, I'll call them. I have a bunch of frequent flyer miles I can use. After I book something, I'll let you know when I'm coming to pick you up."

"Okay," she replied weakly, wiping a stray tear away with her hand. "I really do appreciate your help." Kate was glad she didn't have to go through this alone, realizing that if she hadn't met Ryan by chance on the plane, she would be.

"No problem. I'm pulling up the airline reservation websites right now. I see a direct flight leaving Seattle in a few hours. Hang on."

Kate listened to the sound of Ryan tapping on his keyboard, and then he was back on the phone.

"Okay, I booked a couple of seats on Southwest. The flight leaves in about two and half hours. I'm going to run home and change out of this suit, so I'll be at your place in about forty-five minutes."

"I guess I'd better jump in the shower then. I'll be ready by the time you get here," Kate assured him. "And Ryan..."

"Yes."

"I want you to know you're a godsend."

~*~

The comment about Kerry Park had struck a nerve with Suki—remembering how her parents used to go there to enjoy the view, while she and her brother played on the playground equipment on the terraced level below. Under different circumstances, she would have told Kate so.

What am I going to do now? Suki was flustered at this unexpected turn of events. Her palms began to sweat and her head throbbed, making it hard for her to think clearly.

The plan had been working perfectly—until now. One quick call to Ethan, that's all it would have taken. I could have let him into the storage room before she showed up. He could have taken care of her there, and I wouldn't have had to see it. Suki began to pace the kitchen, frustrated at the possibility of something disrupting her plan. *I had an alibi, and nobody was going to find her for a long time.*

"Ethan's going to be furious." Suki ran a hand through her hair. Kate's leaving would totally screw up Ethan's plan to kill her today. She knew he would certainly be angry about that, maybe even mad at her for not trying to stop Kate from going.

Racking her brain, Suki tried to think of something quick, anything she could do that would keep Kate in Seattle, but her mind went blank. There was nothing. Nothing short of doing the deed herself—right here and now. Only, Suki knew she didn't have it in her. Ethan would have to do his own dirty work.

She glanced down the hallway, to make sure Kate was out of earshot, and then she phoned her brother. Maybe after he cooled down, he could tell her what to do before Kate was out of her grasp. The phone rang several times, but then went to voicemail.

"Ethan, call me back. Kate's leaving town in a few minutes and I don't know what to do. Where are you? I need to talk to you right away. Call me back!"

Suki continued to search her mind for answers, wondering what she could do to keep Kate in town. She decided she would try to overtake her and tie her up. Then her brother could decide what to do with her from there. Rummaging around the kitchen, she found an extension cord in the junk drawer and tiptoed down the hallway to Whitney's room.

As she was trying to decide whether to knock or burst in, she heard Kate talking on the phone. She put her ear to the door and listened.

Ryan. *Well, that changes things.* She returned the cord to the drawer and decided that while Kate was on the phone, she would call her brother again. She was sure Ethan would be furious with Kate's sudden departure, but she needed to alert him to the change of plans.

"Hullo?"

"Ethan, did you get my voicemail?"

"Uh, no. Sorry, I was, uh..."

"Were you out scoring drugs?"

"Never mind. What's going on, Sis?"

"There's been a change of plans. Kate's leaving in a few minutes to go to Boise."

"What? Why?"

"The police called this morning and said the Boise Police want her to look at a dead body they have in their morgue. They think it might be Whitney."

"You know it can't be her."

"I know, but I couldn't tell Kate that. I was going to knock her to the floor and tie her up, but she was on the phone with that guy she met on the plane. It sounds as if he's going with her and he's probably on his way to pick her up. I tried to think of something else, but I just couldn't think of anything that would keep her from going. I'm so stupid!"

"You're not stupid," Ethan said evenly.

It's probably the drugs making him so calm. She knew her brother should be more upset about the change of plans than she was, so she was glad he wasn't giving her a tongue-lashing.

"Just settle down," he told her in a relaxed voice. "Kate will come back to Seattle when she finds out it's not her sister."

"Yeah, I guess you're right."

"We'll have to come up with a different plan. When's she leaving?" he asked.

"I'm not sure but it sounds like soon." Suki peered down the hallway to make sure Kate couldn't overhear her conversation.

"I'm on my way over, and we'll come up with something. She's gonna pay for what she did to Mom and Dad—one way or the other. Call me after she leaves, when the coast is clear."

"Okay."

~*~

Ryan had dropped a few files on his assistant's desk on his way out, but she had stepped away. As he walked out of the elevator, he pulled out his phone and called her.

"Hey, Becky, something's come up and I had to leave for the rest of the day, a personal emergency. Can you get signatures on those addenda I left and forward them to the other agents? I put a few sticky notes on the rest with instructions."

"Sure," she answered.

"I may be out tomorrow, as well. I'm not sure. So, I need you to rearrange the appointments I have on my calendar. If you could go in and check my Outlook to see what I have going that would be a big help."

"Okay. I'll see if Sid can take some of those appointments for you."

"Great," he said.

"What's up?" she asked, a hint of concern in her voice. She had worked for him for the last three years, long enough to know it was not like him just to take off like that.

"I need to fly to Boise this afternoon."

"Didn't you just get back from Boise yesterday?"

"Yes, but I met someone on the plane and—"

"A *female* someone?" she interrupted.

"Yes, a female someone. She's in a bit of a jam and I need to help her out."

"She must be something pretty special for you to just drop everything."

"I'm not dropping everything, just needing to rearrange my plans."

"Still, she must be special," Becky said.

"She is. We had dinner together last night, and I think we really connected. She needs my help, so if I can—"

"Don't worry about a thing, Boss. Sid and I will hold down the fort while you're gone."

"Tha—"

"Hang on a sec. I think you'll want to hear this."

"Hear what?" he asked. He was just about to repeat it when he realized what she meant. In the background, he heard Vanessa's voice. He listened to the exchange.

"I was looking for Ryan. Is he around?"

"Sorry, just missed him."

"Appointment?"

"No."

"When will he be back?"

"Don't know."

"Today?"

Ryan thought that Vanessa sounded like she was getting irritated with Becky's evasiveness. He smiled to himself. He knew Becky didn't like Vanessa—she made no secret of it.

"Probably not."

"Did he go to Boise?" she asked, her voice laden with disgust.

"Can't say."

So, it must have been Vanessa that called in the tip.

He heard Vanessa snort, "*Humph!*" Then he pictured her throwing her long dark tresses over her shoulder, adjusting her fitted suit jacket—eyes narrowed, lips pouting—and storming out. The sound of a slamming door followed by Becky's evil giggle confirmed it.

"Hey, Boss," Becky came back on the line. "So, what were you about to say?"

He chuckled. "Thanks, Beck."

~*~

Kate stuck her head into the kitchen and found Suki seated at the table, reading the morning newspaper.

"Suki, I have to hop in the shower and get ready. I called Ryan and he's going to Boise with me. He'll be coming to pick me up in a little while."

"Really? He hardly knows you."

"True, but I need his help," Kate responded.

"It sounds like he wants something, *if* you know what I mean."

"Suki, it's not like that," Kate replied emphatically, not liking the implication. "He's being a friend. He knows I'm going to need some emotional support when I go in to identify the dead body. I can't exactly call my friends in Los Angeles and have them travel all day. Boise's only an hour's flight from here. I asked Ryan if he'd go with me and he said yes."

"Well, either way, it sounds like you must have had quite an effect on him last night."

Kate smiled to herself and hurried to the bathroom.

She had a quick shower, partially blow-dried her hair and put a little make-up on. Then she slipped into her skinny jeans and a white long-sleeved knit tee, taking her black leather jacket for the ride to the airport, figuring Boise would be much warmer than drizzly Seattle. She packed her small carry-on bag in case they ended up staying overnight.

"Ryan's here!" Suki called out.

Kate met him at the door and they left quickly, not wanting to miss their flight. They hurried the half block to where Ryan had found a prime parking space on the street.

"Listen," Ryan said as they walked toward his Land Rover, "when I was coming to get you, I noticed that guy—the one with the blue ball cap—he was leaning against the far corner of the building."

"You're kidding?"

"No. At first, I wondered if it was him, but when he turned and saw I had seen him, he peeled away from the building and went down the street in the opposite direction. Sorry, but I didn't have time to follow him."

"We'll have to let Patel and Porter know. That guy is turning up just a little too often."

CHAPTER 8

RYAN AND KATE DASHED to the airport. The traffic on the I-5 wasn't too bad, and they were able to nab a choice parking spot in the long-term parking area.

They retrieved their boarding passes from the kiosk. Both Kate and Ryan took their small luggage on board instead of checking them, so they could breeze through the security line.

Once on board, they squeezed into their seats on the small commuter aircraft. Kate was unusually quiet, nervously awaiting take-off. Ryan couldn't help but notice her fidgeting—crossing her arms, then uncrossing them, looking at her watch, shifting in her seat. Her eyes were moist with fear and apprehension.

The plane began to taxi on the runway. As the engines went into full thrust, Kate laid her head back, closed her eyes and gripped the armrests. Once the aircraft leveled out, she released her grasp and let out a long sigh.

"You okay?" Ryan asked.

"I'll be fine," she replied.

Ryan kept light conversation going, talking about the weather and his work. It relaxed her a bit. However, the closer the plane got to Boise, the less talkative Kate became. She felt tense again and kept drifting off, lost in thought.

Ryan must have sensed her anxiety because he reached over and took her hand in his. "Is there anything I can do for you?"

"You're doing it," she said.

With the slightest touch of his index finger, he wiped a stray tear from her cheek.

She met his eyes for a moment, managing a little smile, then turned and looked out the window. She sensed him wanting to keep her engaged in conversation, get her mind on something else, but small talk seemed frivolous right now.

Ryan appeared relieved when the captain's voice came over the loud speaker instructing the flight attendants to prepare the cabin for final descent. Kate noticed him look down at his hand still holding hers. She had found it comforting and had not wanted to let go.

As soon as the plane was on the ground and taxied up to its gate, Ryan and Kate grabbed their carry-ons, disembarked, and hastily made their way to one of the car rental counters. After picking up the car, a white compact sedan, they drove straight to the police headquarters.

Ryan pulled into the parking lot, turned the engine off, and started to reach for the door. Kate laid her hand on his forearm to stop him. He looked surprised, glancing at her hand, and then into her watery eyes.

"Have I told you how much I appreciate you coming with me?"

"Only two or three times," Ryan replied with a grin.

"Well, I just want to make sure you know," she said, doing her best to manage a little smile.

She released her hand and they got out of the car. With his arm draped casually around her shoulders, they briskly walked into the police station and spoke with the receptionist working the front desk. Kate explained to her who she was and why she was there.

"Yes, they're expecting you, Miss McAllister. And who are you, sir?"

"My name is Ryan Wilson. I'm a friend of Kate's."

"All right, then. Let me call an officer to take you to see the Medical Examiner."

She picked up the phone. In a matter of minutes, a female officer appeared. "Just follow me," she said, "and I'll show you where to go."

A couple of detectives were talking outside the door to the morgue as they approached. Their conversation ceased when they saw the trio coming.

"Miss McAllister," the officer said, "this is Detective Gilbert and Detective Franklin. They'll take you inside." The female officer nodded at her colleagues and then left.

"And you are...?" Franklin asked, looking at Ryan.

"I'm Ryan Wilson, a friend of Kate's. I'm here for moral support. I hope you don't mind."

"That's fine. Let's go inside," the detective said.

He pulled open the glass door for them and Kate went through first. She was already a bundle of nerves, and the medicinal and chemical smells made her stomach turn.

The County Medical Examiner was already inside the morgue, waiting for Kate to arrive.

"Doc, this is Kate McAllister," said Detective Gilbert.

Dr. Wagner was a tall, bulky man with a pronounced curvature of the spine, obvious under his white coat, and a full head of gray hair.

"Yes, I've been expecting you," Dr. Wagner said, peering over the top of his wire-rimmed glasses. "So sorry to have to make you do this, but we need to find out who this young woman is. The body is over here," he said as he walked, pointing to the deceased, covered by a large white cloth, lying on a cold metal gurney. "I'll pull back the sheet when you're ready. Just give the word."

Kate steeled herself for the possibility that it was Whitney's lifeless body lying on the steel table. She breathed in slowly and leaned against Ryan for support. He sensed her need and put his arm around her shoulder once more.

"Okay, I'm ready."

Dr. Wagner pulled back the sheet, and Kate gasped. Her stomach lurched. The cold, pale, dead woman was about Whitney's age with similar blonde hair. She had bruises around her neck and a deep wound on her forehead. At first glance, the similarity was disturbing. Kate thought for a panicked moment that it might be Whitney.

"Is it your sister?" Gilbert asked.

"No, it's not." Kate shook her head slightly. "It's not Whitney."

Overcome with relief, her knees went weak and she started to collapse. Ryan grabbed hold of her around the waist to help steady her.

"Why don't you take her out, son? We're done here," the doctor suggested to Ryan, as he covered up the lifeless body.

"Okay, Kate, I've got you. Let's get out of here." With this arm still about her waist, he led her out.

"Thanks, Ryan, I'll be all right," Kate said, as she let him help her out of the room, regaining some strength in her legs. She looked up at Ryan through a blur of tears. "It's upsetting, but I'm glad it's not my sister."

"Me, too," he responded.

Then she turned and looked again at the covered body through the closed glass doors. "It's just so sad, though."

"The girl?" Ryan asked.

"Yes. She's not Whitney, but she was somebody's daughter."

~*~

"Now what?" Kate asked Ryan, standing in front of the police station in the bright sunshine.

"I'll have to check for return flights. I didn't make any reservations because I didn't know what we'd find here and when we'd be returning." He looked at his watch. "It's almost three o'clock. There may still be an available flight back to Seattle tonight. Let me go online and check."

"I need to sit down and get something to eat. I haven't eaten anything since breakfast." Her stomach had been in knots most of the day, and viewing the dead body had drained her emotionally.

"If I remember correctly, I think there's a Starbucks or something not far from here," Ryan said.

"A Chai latté and a slice of pumpkin bread would make me feel better."

Ryan opened the car door for Kate and helped her in, before sliding behind the wheel.

Kate looked over at him, warmth enveloping her like a favorite blanket. She barely knew Ryan—it had only been two days—but he had stepped up and become her knight in shining armor. She normally liked to think of herself as strong and self-reliant, living on her own, running her own business, taking care of herself. Yet these last few days had thrown things at her that she had never had to deal with before.

They drove into the parking lot of the coffee shop and stepped inside.

"Why don't you go up and order something, and I'll find us a table and start checking with the airlines," he said.

"All right. Can I get you anything?" Kate offered, as Ryan took a seat at one of the small tables.

"A bottle of water would be good."

"Okay," Kate said, "I'll be right back.

Leaving Ryan to go online to check the various airline schedules on his smartphone, she went to the counter. As she waited her turn in line, she wondered if there would be any seats left on any of the direct evening flights back to Seattle, with such short notice.

"Any luck?" she asked, setting his water down in front of him. She hoped she wasn't becoming a burden. Surely, he had worked to get back to.

"No. Not any direct flights, anyway. I don't really want to go to Las Vegas and Portland just so I can get back to

Seattle by midnight tonight." A mischievous smile formed on his lips. "I have an idea."

"What?"

"I'm going to call my parents. We can stay at their house tonight and catch an early flight out in the morning."

"They won't mind?" Kate asked.

"Mind? Heck no," he chuckled. "They've been hoping I'd come home with a nice girl for years."

Kate laughed for the first time all day, and it felt good. Then, the realization that her sister was still missing settled over her and she got serious again. "Do you think we should call Detective Patel, or Porter, and let them know the dead woman wasn't my sister?"

"That's a good idea. Why don't you call them while I make these reservations real quick for the morning flights," Ryan said, as he reviewed the screen on his phone, "and then I'll call my folks."

"Okay," she agreed.

Kate dialed Porter's cell number, and he picked up on the first ring.

"This is Detective Porter."

"Detective, this is Kate McAllister."

"Yes, hello, Kate."

"I'm in Boise right now. I flew down here to identify a body the police found yesterday. They thought it might be Whitney's."

"Yes, I heard you were going there."

"But, it wasn't Whitney."

"Yes, I heard that, too. The Boise Police already called here and talked to Patel."

"Hopefully that means she's still alive, don't you think?" Kate was desperate for an encouraging word.

"Let's hope you're right. We have the computer tech going through Whitney's computer again, in case we missed anything, although right now nothing seems out of the ordinary. We've interviewed co-workers and friends from the information her roommate provided, but we haven't turned up anything yet."

"I'll be back on an early morning flight, and you have my number. Please, Detective, call me if you have even the tiniest bit of news. Okay?"

"Will do, Kate," Porter assured her before hanging up.

Where are you, Whitney?

Ryan had overheard her conversation. "I'm sure Raj and Will are doing all they can to find Whitney. There's nothing more we can do right now."

"You're right," she reluctantly agreed, as she tucked her phone in her pocket, "but waiting is just so darn hard."

"I made the flight reservations for seven-thirty in the morning, so that's taken care of," he assured her. "Now, I'll call my folks and let them know we're coming over. They'll be thrilled. I'm sure my mom would love to make a nice dinner for us, and then you can kick your shoes off and relax."

"That sounds so good right now," Kate said, rubbing her temple with a couple of fingers. She could feel a tension headache coming on. Then she reached across the small table, put her hand on his and looked tenderly into his eyes. "I don't know what I would have done without your help."

"You're welcome," Ryan replied, putting his other hand warmly over hers. "I understand that this thing with your sister is not over. So, once we get back to Seattle, if you still need me..."

CHAPTER 9

RYAN HIT SPEED DIAL 1 ON his phone. "It's ringing."

Kate smiled and nodded.

"Hey, Mom. It's Ryan. I'm in Boise." He paused for her response. "Yes, Mom, I know I was just here yesterday." He looked at Kate and raised his eyebrows playfully. "I'm coming over in a few minutes, and I'll explain it then."

Kate watched contentedly as Ryan spoke with his mother. "Yes, everything is all right. Nothing you need to be troubled about. I'll see you in a little while. Don't worry."

Kate smiled, wishing she still had a mother she could tell not to worry. She gazed wistfully at Ryan.

"Oh, and, Mom, I have a friend with me. We'll need to spend the night. Is that okay?" Ryan asked. Another pause. "Kate." He winked at her. "Yes, Mom, a girl. But it's not what you think. I'll explain when we get there."

"Yes, you can tell Dad. Bye, love you."

Ryan shut off his phone as he stood and stuck it in his coat pocket. A wide grin spread across his lips.

Kate could tell from his side of the conversation that he had a close relationship with his parents. The longer she was with this man, the more she liked him. She stared at him with the beginning of a smile on her face and shook her head.

"What?" he asked.

"Nothing."

"You're staring at me."

"I know." How could she not?

He raised a curious eyebrow. "Okay, then. Let's go get in the car and head over to my folks' place. It's just outside of the little burb of Eagle, not too far from here."

Once in the car, Kate asked Ryan what his mother's response was to him bringing a girl home.

"Just like I told you it would be—she was thrilled," he replied, navigating the vehicle out of the parking lot.

"I enjoyed listening to you talk to your mom. It made me think of my own parents and how much I miss them."

"You said they died in an auto accident, didn't you?" He pulled into the flow of traffic.

"Yes, it was kind of a freak thing."

"What do you mean?"

"The police weren't sure what happened, so they called it an accident and closed the case. My mom and dad had taken the ferry from Seattle over to Bainbridge Island for the day and somehow their car ended up wrapped around a big tree off the main road to Poulsbo. The police report said they both died instantly."

"No other cars were involved?"

"No. The police thought maybe they swerved to miss a motorcycle or an animal or something." Kate's throat grew tight and her bottom lip quivered. "No one really knows."

She turned her head to look out the window and wrapped her arms around herself. She didn't want Ryan to see the tears that were filling her eyes—he'd seen enough of them already.

"I'm sorry. It must have been devastating for you and Whitney."

"It was," she replied, still staring out the window.

"I can't even imagine losing my folks."

"I haven't been back to Seattle since then—until this happened, I mean." She sat up straight, blinked back her tears and drew in a deep breath. "I couldn't help my parents, but I hope I can help my sister." She swiveled in her seat to face him. "I can't wait to fly back there in the morning."

"I know you're anxious, but there's nothing we can do tonight. So, let's have some dinner and try to relax."

"You're right, that does sound good." If only she could relax—her stomach was still in knots.

"Raj will call if there's any news," he assured her.

Kate glanced at him and smiled to herself. He seemed to know just what to say and do to make her feel better. She was looking forward to meeting the people that raised this wonderfully caring man, the parents who taught him values, taught him how to treat a woman. *No wonder he wants a family of his own.*

~*~

Ryan drove through the small town of Eagle. Kate was pleasantly surprised by the quaint shops and upscale feel of the main street. They continued on the street leading out of town, which took them into a rural area.

"Your Mom and Dad live in the country?"

"Yep. They live on a ten-acre horse property just up the road a little ways. Hey, do you like horses?"

"I do. I didn't grow up around horses in Seattle, of course, but in L.A. I have friends who have horses and I get to ride them occasionally." Well, maybe not friends exactly, more like close acquaintances. Perhaps it was the superficial clients she worked with or the self-absorbed people she had met, but she had found it difficult to make many genuine friends in that city.

"I'll have to show you ours."

"I'd like that," she replied. At least she hoped she would.

Ryan turned in at the white vinyl fencing, pulling onto the long paved driveway leading back to the house. At the end of the driveway sat an older two-story farmhouse that looked like it had been remodeled recently. The house was painted a pale yellow with white trim and black shutters. The walkway leading up to the expansive front porch was bordered with small green shrubs and flowering plants. Beyond the farmhouse were several outbuildings and a large red barn.

It was so picturesque that Kate reached in her purse for her camera to capture it all. Instead, poking around in her bag, she discovered it wasn't there. It rattled her. She realized that, in her rush to leave Seattle, she had unintentionally left her camera sitting on the bed.

"Shoot! I forgot my camera." Kate exclaimed.

"It's okay."

"You don't understand. I *never* forget my camera. *Ever.*"

"Calm down. Do you remember where you left it?" Ryan asked.

"Yes, on Whitney's bed."

"It'll still be there when you get back."

"I know, but I feel naked without it." The camera represented the one thing in her life she could control.

Before Ryan and Kate were out of the car, his folks came out onto the front porch, ready to greet their son and his new friend. Ryan's mom was a short, chubby woman with shoulder-length blonde hair. She stood next to his dad—tall, lean and dark haired, wearing rimless glasses. Their black and white border collie pranced eagerly next to them.

"Hello, you guys!" Ryan's mom called out as she waved from the porch. "Need any help with anything?" The dog ran down the steps to meet them.

"No, we've got it, Mom." He grabbed the bags.

"Good boy," Ryan said to the dog, whose tail was wagging energetically. Ryan crouched down to greet him and rubbed his head. "Hey, Riley, this is Kate." As if Riley understood the introduction, he ran over to Kate to sniff the new guest.

"Hey there, Riley," Kate said, as the dog jumped up and planted his paws on her abdomen.

"Riley, come!" Ryan's dad ordered firmly, in response to the dog's overly enthusiastic greeting of their guest. The dog immediately obeyed and bounded up the steps to the porch.

"Sit," Ryan's dad commanded, and he did.

Then Ryan climbed the few steps up to the porch and gave his mom a hug and then his dad. He turned and revealed Kate who followed right behind him.

"Mom, Dad, this is Kate."

"Kate, it's so good to meet you. I'm Jeanie," Ryan's mom gave her a quick hug, which surprised Kate. "And this is Jack."

"Yes, it's nice to meet you, Kate," Ryan's dad added, extending his hand. "Sorry about the dog. He gets so excited when anyone new comes by."

"No problem," Kate shook his hand. "I love dogs."

"Well, let's go inside. No need to keep standing out here," Jeanie ordered, leading the way.

Once inside, Kate instantly felt at home. The décor of the house was warm and inviting with dark wide-plank hardwood floors, leather furniture and rich earth-tone fabrics. There was a large stone fireplace in the great room, already stocked with cut wood and kindling, ready to start a roaring fire.

The new-looking kitchen opened up to a comfortable living area, a granite-topped center island divided the two rooms. This was more than Kate expected from a farmhouse, and she was impressed by the beauty of it all.

"Your home is lovely, Mrs. Wilson," Kate said as they entered the kitchen area and stood around the island.

"Please, Kate, call me Jeanie. Mrs. Wilson is Jack's mother."

"Okay, Jeanie."

"You must be exhausted, dear. I've made up the guest room for you. And Ryan, you'll be in your old room, of course. Unless..."

"Unless what?" Kate asked, looking suspiciously at Ryan, feeling warmth rush to her cheeks.

"It's not like that, Mom," Ryan said, glancing back at Kate.

"Well, anyway," Jeanie explained, "the rooms are made up and ready for you—whatever you decide."

"What's for dinner?" Ryan asked, quickly changing the subject. He looked around the kitchen. "I don't smell anything cooking."

"That's because Dad and I are going out," his mom replied.

"Out?" Ryan seemed surprised they'd be going out when guests were coming to stay.

"We have tickets to the BSU football game tonight. It's a sell out," his dad noted, "and we're not going to miss it. They're playing Virginia Tech."

"The Tomlinsons invited us to tailgate with them before the kick-off. They're grilling burgers and ribs. You remember the Tomlinsons, don't you, Ryan?" Jeanie asked.

"Yes, but..."

"Honey, we do have a life, you know," his mother reminded him. "I left some steaks and chicken in the fridge for you if you'd like to barbecue. There are salad fixings and some leftover *Ooh La La* potatoes in there, too. I know how much you like those."

Kate smiled as she observed the interaction with interest and pleasure. It seemed Ryan, on the other hand, couldn't believe that his mother wasn't preparing dinner for them.

"Oh, Ryan, you're a big boy. You cook your own meals in Seattle, don't you?" Then Jeanie caught herself,

95

apparently afraid she'd said the wrong thing. "Unless Kate cooks for you."

"Yes, Mom, I cook my own dinners, that is, when I'm not going out or picking up take-out. And, no, Kate doesn't cook for me. I told you it's—never mind. I just thought—"

"Well, you thought wrong, honey. Dad and I are leaving shortly, and we'll be back after the game. You'll have the house all to yourselves for a while."

"I'm sorry to interrupt," Kate said, "but I think I'd like to go to my room and freshen up. If someone will just give me a little direction..."

"Sure, hon, top of the stairs, first door on the right," Jeanie responded.

"Thanks."

~*~

When Kate was out of earshot, Ryan's mom and dad grilled him about what was going on and why he was back in Boise with his mysterious friend. Ryan explained that Kate's sister was missing and why she had to make the unscheduled stop in Boise.

"Oh, how awful," his mother said, putting a hand up to her lips.

"What does that have to do with you? Are you dating Kate or what?" his father asked.

"No, Dad, we're not dating. Let me start from the beginning." He explained to them how he had met Kate on the plane to Seattle, just yesterday morning. They were seated across the aisle from each other. She seemed sweet and they had a good conversation. "It appeared to me like we hit it off, but then I lost her before we got to baggage claim."

"Looks like you found her again," his dad kidded.

"Yes, I did." Ryan shook his head at his father's humor. He went on to explain how he had reconnected with her outside of the police station. That was when Kate told him her sister was missing. She confessed to him that was the real reason why she was in Seattle. "Since she doesn't know anyone there, I've been trying to help her out and be supportive."

"I don't understand. Why did you bring her to Boise?" Jeanie asked.

"Well, maybe you saw the story on the news about a young woman's body being found by the Boise River," Ryan went on to say.

"Yes, I think I did hear something about that. Was that her sister?" Jeanie asked sympathetically.

"No, thank goodness, but that's why Kate flew to Boise this afternoon. The police asked her to come and see if it was her missing sister. I came for moral support."

"I see," his father replied.

"We've become friends over these last days, and she needed someone to lean on, to help her get through this. She has no family left, other than her sister."

"Poor thing," his mother said.

"So you're just friends, huh?" Jack inquired. "She's awfully pretty."

"Yes, we're just friends, Dad." He met his father's gaze. "I'd be lying if I said I haven't begun to feel more for her than that, because I have. She's so much more than just a pretty face, Dad."

Ryan stepped alongside his mother and put his arm around her shoulder. "You know, she's smart and she's funny, and she has her own photography business in L.A."

"She sounds wonderful." Jeanie smiled.

"She is." Then Ryan looked his father in the eye again. "Except, Dad, she's in an emotionally vulnerable place right now, and I don't want to take advantage of her."

"Good for you, honey." Jeanie patted Ryan's hand that rested on her shoulder. "I'm glad to see we raised you right. It sounds like Kate really needs a friend she can rely on right now."

"Take care of that girl," his dad said. "She sounds like a keeper."

"Yes, dear," Jeanie remarked, "a keeper."

Jack glanced down at his watch. "Holy smokes! We've got to go now, Jeanie. Bob and Cathy will be wondering where we are. And I'd hate to see him burn those ribs on our account."

"Okay, okay, just let me grab my purse," she said as she came around the kitchen island to retrieve it. She stopped in front of Ryan, reached up, and put a hand on his cheek. "You and Kate have a nice evening together, all right?"

"Sure thing, Mom."

~*~

While Kate was off to Boise, Suki thought she had better check on Whitney again and feed her more sleeping pills. With the delay, it was on her to keep Whitney sequestered and asleep, which was increasingly difficult as the extra days kept piling on. Aggravated that things had not gone according to plan, she set about making yet another special peanut butter sandwich for her captive.

Frustrated, Suki furiously ground a small handful of sleeping pills into a fine powder and mixed them into the peanut butter. Then she hastily spread it on the bread, adding a layer of blackberry jam on top to mask the bitter chemical taste and make it go down easier.

And then Ethan was supposed to get rid of Kate on Monday, she mumbled to herself, as she rifled through the crowded utensil drawer for a knife. *After that, Ethan and I would have left town and disappeared. But noooo! Here it is Wednesday, the deed's not done and Kate's gone off to Boise!*

Irritated and distracted, she grabbed at a knife and accidentally sliced her index finger open. "Ow!" Bright red blood oozed out of the gash. Wrapping a kitchen towel around her hand, she ran to the bathroom to put a bandage on it.

Great! That's all I need. One more thing going wrong. She hurriedly dressed the cut and went back to the kitchen to bag up the sandwich and leave.

Suki took the bus downtown to the Underground Tour. Even though she had a car, taking the bus was so much more economical and convenient because of the lack of parking in the downtown area. Plus, this way, there would be no vehicle for anybody to notice and trace back to her.

As the bus rolled along, she stared out the window, pondering what she and her brother were doing. *If Ethan had his way, he'd just let Whitney die. But, it wasn't Whitney's fault. It was Kate's.*

Suki had a soft spot for Whitney. From the first time Suki answered her ad for a roommate, there was an easy friendliness between them. She thought Whitney was sweet and fun to be around, which made it easy for Suki to fulfill her part of the plan.

Whitney never realized she had gone to junior high with Suki. They weren't friends back then, although they did share some classes. Whitney was one of the popular girls, not because she had money or was a cheerleader, or anything like that, but because she was outgoing and pretty, and she was friendly to almost everyone.

Suki, on the other hand, had been one of the quiet girls with her mousy brown hair and a few extra pounds, one of those girls who blended into the background. She only had a couple of girls she would call friends. Back then, she and her friends wished they were Whitney, but all that changed one fateful day when Suki lost her mother.

The city bus came to an abrupt stop at Pioneer Square and the doors slid open as the air brakes let out a *whoosh*. Suki stepped off the bus and started for her destination. The noisy bus pulled away, leaving her in a cloud of nauseating exhaust fumes.

As she pulled a large gray scarf out of her purse, a light rain began falling. She tied it on her head to hide her red curls and shield her from the rain.

She hurried across the street and entered the building through the heavy wooden doors leading to the Underground Tour. She immediately turned to the right and hurried down the old, painted green steps to the Rogues Gallery souvenir shop in the lower level, hoping none of her co-workers would notice her.

Since a tour of about thirty people had just ended, the shop was fairly full. The tour visitors going into the souvenir shop was the finale. Suki kept her head down and tried to look as inconspicuous as possible as she filed through the shop and back into the underground city.

Reaching the place where the old blue Dino's diner sign leaned against the locked door, she pulled it away and let herself in, closing it gingerly behind her. With her flashlight in hand, she carefully trod to the back of the room where Whitney lay tied up and asleep on the dirty old bed.

"Whitney, wake up." Suki shook her shoulder and shined the light on her face. Whitney did not move. Suki swallowed hard as a shot of adrenaline jumped through her veins.

"Whitney! I said, wake up!" She shook her more vigorously and yanked the tape off her mouth with a *rip*.

"Ouch! What, what's going on?" Whitney snapped blearily out of her sleep.

Suki exhaled forcefully. "Sit up, Whitney," she ordered, as she untied her feet. Whitney was too out of it. "I brought you something to eat, but you need to sit up."

"What? What's happening?" Whitney slurred.

"You need to eat something. Please sit up." Suki knew she had to get the sleeping pills into Whitney once more, one way or the other. It wasn't Whitney's fault she was in this place, but Suki had to do what had to be done. She had no intention of either her or Ethan going to jail.

"Leave me...*alone*. I'm tired. Jus' wanna...sleep," Whitney stammered.

"Here, let me help you sit up."

"No. I jus' wanna sleep." Her words were slow and garbled.

Whitney wasn't cooperating and Suki was getting desperate. She took the sandwich out of her purse and pulled the slices of bread apart to expose the peanut butter. She threw the jam side on the ground. Then she scraped the drug-filled peanut butter off the bread with her finger. She pried Whitney's mouth open and shoved the peanut butter inside, holding her mouth closed so she would swallow it all.

Whitney coughed and sputtered, attempting to shake her head away, but Suki held tight. Suki's bandage worked loose from her finger as she struggled to hold Whitney's mouth shut. The gash reopened and began to bleed again.

Finally, Whitney gave in and swallowed the peanut butter, gasping for air as it stuck in her throat.

"Drink this!" Suki gave her a sip of water from the partial bottle she had brought, pouring the rest on her fingers to wash off the blood.

Once Whitney was breathing okay, she put more tape over her mouth and laid her back down to sleep, retying her feet to the bed. Pulling a couple of tissues out of the packet in her purse, she wound them around her finger to contain the bleeding. She left the way she came in and slipped out of the souvenir shop undetected.

Catching the city bus, she rode it home, deep in thought, wondering if she and her brother were doing the right thing. It wasn't fair Whitney had to suffer for Kate's sins, but Ethan didn't see it that way. He only saw Whitney as a means to his end.

When she stepped off the bus at her stop, she saw Ethan waiting for her by the entrance to her apartment building. She dug into her oversized purse and pulled out her set of keys.

"Hi, Ethan," she said as she pushed the key into the lock and opened the building's front door.

"Hey," he replied, looking up and down the street, before following her through the foyer and into the elevator.

"What's that on your finger?" he asked, noticing the tissue wrapped around it.

"Oh, I cut myself earlier and it started bleeding again," she explained.

"Is it bad?"

"No, not too."

Once inside the loft, Suki hung her purse on one of the coat hooks by the door and shrugged out of her trench coat, hooking it on the coat rack, as well.

Ethan settled into an overstuffed chair in the living area and removed his ball cap, exposing his unruly brown hair. He stuck his feet up on the small, well-worn coffee table to relax and leaned his head back.

"I'm going to go and put another bandage on my finger. I'll be right back," she called as she walked down the hallway to the bathroom.

"Did you check on Whitney?" he hollered.

She re-bandaged her finger and headed back. "Yes," she replied as she walked into the room.

"Do you think anyone saw you there?" He scratched his head and ran his hand through his thick, wavy hair.

"No, I was very careful."

"How was she? Still breathing?"

"Yes, she's still breathing. I had to force-feed the sleeping pills to her today, but I got them down her. I thought you didn't care about her."

"I don't."

"Then why all the questions?"

"If she has to die for me to get to Kate, so be it. On the other hand, if something gets messed up, we can use her as leverage. So, it's to our advantage to keep her alive as long as we need her. After that, who freakin' cares?"

Suki was taken aback by how cold Ethan had become. He was so far from the funny and sweet brother she had grown up with years ago. Since the tragedy that shattered their family, she had watched her brother change as he spiraled down into depression and addiction to drugs and alcohol. Aside from looking to score his next fix, his whole life was now focused on getting his revenge.

CHAPTER 10

KATE CHANGED INTO SOMETHING more comfortable. She came down the stairs in her jeans and tennis shoes and found Ryan at the kitchen island preparing dinner. The salad was made, and the potatoes were warming in the oven. The steak and chicken breasts were marinating in a glass pan on the counter. *I guess I was right,* she thought to herself, *he is the perfect man.*

"Mmmm...something smells good," she said as she strolled into the kitchen.

"That would be my mom's Ooh La La potatoes," Ryan answered with a smile.

"Ooh La La potatoes? What's that?"

"Oh, it's just some delicious potato concoction my mother makes on special occasions."

"What's in it? Besides potatoes, I mean."

"Butter, sour cream, cheddar cheese, green onions. You know, healthy stuff like that," he replied with a smirk.

"Sounds delicious. Can I help with anything?"

"Well, I was thinking that before it gets too late I should take you to see the horses."

"But what about dinner?"

"It'll keep. Let me just turn the oven temperature down real low on these potatoes and they'll be fine. The grill is heating up outside, but it won't hurt anything to just leave it going for a while. Here, let's go out this way." Ryan opened the French doors from the dining area to the patio and let Kate through the doorway first.

As she stepped out into the backyard, she stopped on the patio to take in the view. The sun was setting in the distance, acres of green grass and trees, cordoned off with white fencing surrounded the red barn that looked freshly painted. She found the country air and the picturesque view rejuvenating.

She noticed Ryan watching her, as her face and body relaxed. "This is absolutely breathtaking."

"Yes, it is pretty great." He moved closer. "I don't want to rush you, but it will be dark soon."

"Lead the way."

Riley had been lying on the patio, and he sprang up, eager to go with them. Ryan took hold of Kate's hand and led her to the pasture. Riley wagged his tail all the way.

They stopped at the fence and waited for the horses to approach. There were five of them in the pasture, a variety of colors. A blonde one with a white crest on her head and a chestnut mare trotted over.

"They're magnificent," Kate remarked, once again wishing she had brought her camera.

"It's getting too dark for a ride. Maybe some other time," he suggested.

She understood what he implied, that he hoped she might be there with him again sometime. "I'd like that." She stroked the chestnut mare's long nose and patted her on the neck. The other horse muscled her way in between Kate's hand and the chestnut mare, and nudged her forearm so she would pet her too.

"Looks like someone wants your attention all to herself," Ryan teased.

"It sure looks that way." Kate rubbed the horse's jaw.

Ryan stepped in closer and stroked the golden horse's nose. "I can't say I blame her."

Kate could feel Ryan's body almost touching hers, and it made her heart beat faster. She slowly turned her head and looked up into his deep green eyes. He caught her gaze and held it for a moment.

She sensed he might lean down and kiss her, but he took a small step back and petted the mare. Awkwardly, she blinked and looked back at the horses.

Her heart was beating hard now. Kate could feel the blood pulsing throughout her body. She wanted him to kiss her. *Did I misread the look in his eyes? Is he not as attracted to me as I am to him?*

It had only been two days since they met, yet they were two emotionally intense days of close contact. She was finding him to be everything she had ever wanted in a man. *Did I misinterpret his cues? Maybe it's too soon, but it would only be a kiss.*

"Are you ready to head back to the house?" Ryan asked. "I should probably put the meat on the grill before it gets too late."

"You're right, it's almost dark."

They turned and headed back toward the house, the dog leading the way. Ryan reached down and took her hand again in his as they walked. Now, she was really confused.

Once inside the house, they set about making supper.

"Steak or chicken breast?" he asked her.

"I'll have the chicken. And while you're at the grill, I'll set the table."

"Sounds good." He jabbed a fork in the steak, and then the chicken, before laying them on a plate and seasoning them. "I'll be back shortly," he said as he started out the door to the patio. "The potatoes should be done and the salad is in the refrigerator."

"What about drinks?" Kate asked.

"Check the fridge. There should be wine, soda, sweet tea, bottled water...I'm guessing. Pick whatever you like. I'll just have some sweet tea," he said, as he closed the door behind him.

~*~

Ryan stood before the hot grill. The meats sizzled as he laid them on it. As the meat cooked, he peered back through the French doors into the lighted house and watched Kate set the table. She looked so at home there, and he wondered what it would be like to have a wife like her, a partner, a woman to come home to every night—that was beautiful both inside and out—a woman that would warm their home.

He had come so close to kissing her just a few minutes before. With every cell of his body, he wanted to do it. He was drawn to her like he had never been drawn to any other woman, but as he looked into her eyes he remembered what he told his parents before they left, that he would not take advantage of her. Recalling that conversation pulled him back.

He sensed she wanted him to kiss her—he read it in her eyes—but he knew, because of what she had just gone through at the morgue, and continued to go through as she waited for news of her sister, she was vulnerable. If she had kissed him, he knew there was no way he could have refused, but he didn't want to be the one to initiate things.

They hadn't spoken of her sister in the last hour or so, but he was sure Whitney was never far from Kate's mind. He knew, because she wasn't far from his, either.

~*~

As Kate laid the last fork down and poured the iced tea, she surveyed the well-appointed kitchen and the inviting great room. This house made her feel comfortable and settled. She wondered what it would be like to have a home like this and a family of her own.

When her tasks were finished, Kate stepped out onto the patio with a clean platter. "Mmmm...smells good."

"Thanks," he replied, taking the plate from her. "It's almost done."

She felt his gaze follow her back inside the house. She wondered if he was as distracted by thoughts of the last few days as she was. The smell of burning meat answered her question.

"Oh, man!" she heard him blurt out.

She turned to see him quickly scrape the meat off the grill. He wore a look of embarrassment as he brought his burnt offerings into the house on the platter.

"I hope you like your chicken well done," he said, holding out the large dish for her to see his blunder.

"Oh, my," she giggled and took a seat at the table. "I guess it isn't anything a good bottle of barbeque sauce won't fix."

"Sorry about that." He grabbed the barbeque sauce from the cupboard. "The time just got away from me, I guess," he said sheepishly. He set the platter down on the table and took a seat, too.

Over dinner, Ryan shared with Kate what it was like growing up in Boise, and she described her years being raised in Seattle, then going off to college in California. The conversation was pleasant and upbeat, but thoughts of Whitney niggled in the back of her mind. Likely Ryan's too, for she could tell he was stepping around the subject of her sister, guessing he didn't want to risk upsetting her. And Kate, too, avoided talking about Whitney, reluctant to dampen the mood.

She still felt a little guilty about enjoying Ryan's company when her sister might be struggling for her life somewhere, but as he had reminded her earlier, there was nothing they could do tonight but wait for word from the police.

"That was really good, Ryan." She placed her fork across her plate.

"Mmmm, yes it was. I'm stuffed," he replied as he patted his stomach. "I guess I didn't burn the meat too badly."

"No room for dessert?"

"Maybe later. There's probably ice cream in the freezer. Mom always keeps a couple of flavors for my dad."

Kate stood and began to pick up their dishes.

"Here, let me get that," Ryan offered. He took the plates and glasses to the sink while Kate picked up the salad bowl and half-empty baking dish and came to stand beside him at the sink.

"Those potatoes were so delicious. I'll have to get the recipe from your mom."

"I'm sure she'll be happy to share it."

"I'll get the stuff into the dishwasher, Ryan. Why don't you go and sit down? I will just be a minute."

"Okay, if you don't need me." He moved to the great room and was about to take a seat when he saw the logs and kindling. "Hey, it looks like Dad got the fireplace ready to light. Would you like a fire tonight?"

"That would be wonderful," Kate answered from the kitchen, thinking about how warm and cozy it would make that room. A roaring fire was one thing she missed about living in her condo in Southern California.

"Do you mind if we watch a little of the Boise State game on TV? Most likely it's more than half over by now, but I'd like to see if my alma mater is ahead."

"Sure," she replied, smiling down at the dishes she was sticking in the dishwasher. Kate could hardly believe how comfortable and at home she felt in this house—and with Ryan.

She watched him click on the widescreen TV with the remote control and find the ESPN channel. There before her eyes was the bright blue turf of Boise State. She could see it vividly from where she stood.

She finished cleaning up before joining him on the sofa and enjoying the blazing fireplace. "You weren't kidding when you said the turf was blue," she said from the kitchen, getting no response from Ryan.

"Ryan." She spoke a little louder, moving toward the great room.

"Yeah?" he responded, intently focused on the game.

"You weren't kidding when you said the turf was blue." She laughed as she walked over to sit down next to him. "It's kind of Smurf blue, isn't it?"

"You didn't believe me, did you?" he teased.

"Well, what's the score?" she asked, changing the subject.

"Boise State 21, Virginia Tech 14. They're just one touchdown apart."

"Go Boise!" she declared, pumping a fist in the air, wanting to sound like she was supporting Ryan's team. In truth, she knew very little about football. The sum total of her football knowledge was that she knew when a touchdown was made and that there was usually a kick for the extra point after, but simply rooting for the home team seemed fun and a nice diversion.

"Woo hoo! Go Broncos!" Ryan called out in response to a great play his team just made. "I'll bet Mom and Dad are having a great time at the game. They love their Broncos."

Then Virginia Tech scored again, and the game was tied. It was early in the fourth quarter. Boise State got the ball, pulled off what Ryan explained was a Statue of Liberty play, known as a *trickeration*, and the receiver made an unexpected beeline to their end zone and scored. *Touchdown!*

Kate and Ryan were on their feet cheering. Their lead didn't last long as Virginia Tech scored again, tying the game once more.

With only thirty-five seconds left on the clock, Boise needed to score again to win. Otherwise, they would be going into overtime. Kate was getting into the game with the help of Ryan's play-by-play announcing. She had a death grip on his forearm as the ball was hiked to BSU's quarterback. He threw the ball to one of the receivers, apparently with the precision of a surgeon. The ball was caught near Boise's ten-yard line and the receiver ran it in for a touchdown with only three seconds left on the clock.

Kate and Ryan jumped to their feet again, whooping and hollering with excitement as Boise State won. She threw her arms around his neck and kissed him. He started to put his arms around her, but then she let go, not sure if she should have done that.

He looked surprised, as if he was wondering what to do next.

Kate decided she liked kissing him—it felt right. So, she eased her arms back around his neck and kissed him again, letting him envelop her in his arms this time. He returned the kiss, first softly, then deeply.

Their embrace was interrupted by the jangling sound of Kate's phone ringing in her pocket. Her first thought was that it might be news about Whitney. Ryan let go of her and she hurried to answer it.

"Hello, this is Kate."

"Hi, this is Detective Porter."

"Is there any news?"

"Well, the computer tech was going through your sister's computer a second time and I think we may have found something."

"What?"

"I'm not sure that it means anything, but my gut is telling me it might. It's a photo Whitney had saved on her computer as 'Suki & guy.' It looks like she snapped a picture of a worn old photo with her phone, so it's not real sharp. The tech didn't think it meant anything earlier, when he was scrolling through the files. However, tonight I was standing over his shoulder when the file came up in her list of saved photos, and I recalled that yellow sticky note we found in your sister's room. Remember? The one that said 'Suki & guy' with a question mark on it?"

"Yes, I remember that. What do you suppose it means?"

"I don't really know. I thought maybe you could take a look at the picture and tell us. Is there a computer where you're staying? I thought I could email the photo to you."

"Let me check." She turned to Ryan. "Detective Porter has a photo he wants to email to me. Is there a computer here I can use?"

"Sorry, Dad took it to the shop for repairs when I was here last weekend."

"No, Detective Porter, there isn't a computer here," she said.

"Hmm," Porter responded. "I wonder if there's any other way to get it to you."

"What about my iPhone?" Ryan suggested. "He could email it to me." He quickly wrote on a scrap of paper.

Kate picked up the paper. "Okay. You can send it to my friend Ryan's email address, and he'll get it on his phone. Send it to *Ryan at RyanWilsonHomes*—all one word—*dot com*."

"I can do that," the detective responded. Kate could hear the clicking of the keyboard strokes in the background. "I'm sending it now. You should have it in just a minute."

"Okay, here it comes," Ryan said. He opened the email attachment and handed Kate his phone so she could see.

The image came up on the screen, but the photo was too small and fuzzy to identify the people in it. If it had been a close-up photo, it would have been easier. Unfortunately, it was a full body shot that had been taken from a distance. Plus, it didn't help that it was a photo of a well-worn picture either.

"I'm sorry, but I can't tell from this little picture. The faces are too tiny," she told Detective Porter.

Ryan reached over. "I can spread it out and make it larger. See if this is better," Ryan said as he used his fingers to spread the photo diagonally, zooming in.

"No, that made it grainy," Kate said. "I wish I could see it on a full-size computer screen."

"Is there anybody else you know in town who has a computer?" Porter asked.

Kate repeated the question to Ryan.

"It's pretty late here, Kate. This town rolls up the sidewalks at ten," Ryan said. "Besides, if it's that tattered, I'm not sure if that would help."

She explained it to the detective.

"When will you be back in Seattle?" Porter asked.

"We have a flight out early tomorrow morning," she replied.

"That'll have to do."

"I'll come to the police station directly from the airport, about nine o'clock. I can take a look at it then."

"Okay. Try to get some rest and we'll see you in the morning. Goodnight," the detective said.

Kate clicked off her phone and sat down on the sofa. Then Ryan sat beside her.

"Do you know what this means, Ryan? This is the first lead in the case. If I can identify the people in the photo, it might help get my sister back." She was talking fast, her spirit was energized and her mind was racing. She hadn't even had a moment to process the kiss, and now this possible break in the case.

"Yeah, I agree. It could be an important piece in figuring out who took your sister and why," Ryan said.

"Yes, exactly. If the police can figure that out, then there's more of a chance of finding her alive and getting her back, don't you think?"

"Yeah, I do."

She shot up off the couch and onto her feet. "I have to do something," she said, shaking her hands. "I'm just so excited. I can't sit still."

He noticed the dog whimpering at the French doors to be let outside. Ryan stood too, and he took one of her wiggly hands in his.

"Why don't we take the dog for a little walk?" he suggested.

"Okay, let me grab my jacket." She sprinted up the stairs to her guest room while Ryan and Riley waited.

"All set," Kate announced as she returned.

Riley darted outside as soon as Ryan opened the door. He flipped the back lights on and followed Kate out.

They strolled out to the fence along the pasture once again to see the horses in the moonlight. A black horse trotted over to the fence and Ryan put his hand out to pet her neck.

Kate reached out and stroked her long nose. "She's a beauty."

"I think she's my mom's favorite."

"Maybe your mother will let me ride her some time."

"Maybe," Ryan replied, winking at Kate.

"It's so peaceful out here. Nothing like L.A."

"I'm sure L.A. has some good points, no?"

"Yes, a few, but nothing like this," she said, gazing up at the sky. "I can actually see the stars out here."

Riley ran up between them and barked a couple of times.

"He's telling us he wants to go inside now," Ryan interpreted.

"What a smart dog," Kate remarked. "Okay, boy, let's go!"

Ryan took her hand in his again as they walked back to the house, as if it was the most natural thing in the world.

Once inside, Ryan checked on the fire, crouching down to poke at the embers and add a couple more logs to it.

Kate stood by him, content watching him work. "I really have enjoyed this evening, Ryan, probably more than any other I've had in a very long time."

He stood up and turned to face her.

"I'm glad to hear that," he replied, running his hand lightly down her arm and taking her hand in his. "Now, don't you think we ought to talk about what happened before the walk, before your phone rang?"

"What happened before my phone rang? Oh, yes, what *was* that?" she asked playfully, looking up into his adoring eyes.

"I believe it would be called a kiss." His lips curled into an impish smile as he looked down at her.

"I wasn't planning to do it," she explained. "I've never been one to kiss a guy first. It just…happened. It was one of those spontaneous things."

"I'm glad you did."

"Me, too," Kate agreed.

"I really wanted to kiss you out by the horses when we were out there the first time, but I thought I'd better not."

"Why not?"

"With everything that's going on with your sister, I just thought... well, I didn't want to take advantage of you, Kate. But I'm so attracted to you that I can hardly stand it."

"I was starting to wonder. I thought maybe it was just me." She pushed herself up on her tiptoes and happily planted another kiss on his warm lips. He started to slip his arms around her, but he stopped short, hearing an untimely squeak from the front door opening. Their heads turned in unison toward the noise.

~*~

"Hello! We're home!" his mother called out as she and his dad came through the front door.

Ryan and Kate abruptly stepped apart and laughed at yet another interruption.

He could tell his mom had an inkling there was more to the *we're just friends* spin he was trying to sell her before they left. He appreciated her giving them sufficient warning that someone was walking in on them.

"What are you two giggling about?" Jeanie asked, setting her purse down on the counter as Jack helped her take her coat off.

"Oh, nothing," Ryan answered, like a guilty schoolboy caught red-handed, trying to hide his mischief.

"Yeah, I'm sure it was nothing," Jeanie smirked.

Ryan could tell his mother thought there might be something going on while she and his dad were out of the house. And, he knew she'd be pleased that her son might have finally found a great girl. *Vanessa the Shark,* as his mom liked to call her, had always rubbed her the wrong way.

She whispered something to Ryan's father as she gently jabbed her elbow in his side. Ryan figured it had something to do with him and Kate.

His father changed the subject fast, confirming Ryan's suspicions. "Hey, did you guys catch the game on TV?" he asked as he moved to the great room and sunk down into his oversized leather chair. He put his feet up on the matching ottoman and leaned back.

"Yeah, we saw the last quarter. It was great," Ryan answered.

"I even enjoyed it, though I've never been much for football," Kate said as she directed her attention to Ryan's father. "I have to say, it was an exciting game, at least the part we saw. We were cheering and jumping up and down."

"I know what you mean," Ryan's dad said, "the crowd in the stands was going wild, too."

"And Ryan had told me about the crazy blue turf yesterday, but I thought he was kidding until I saw it for myself," Kate added.

"We love our blue turf," his mom declared, sounding proud of it.

"It's definitely different," said Kate.

"Well, I'm glad you guys had a good time. Did you do anything else?" Jeanie asked, obviously fishing for details.

"As a matter of fact, we did. We took a walk out to the pasture, and I showed Kate the horses. Then we came back and made dinner before we watched the end of the game."

"Sounds like a nice evening. You know, it's not very late. Would anyone care for some coffee or dessert?" Jeanie offered.

"Not me, thank you," Kate replied. "We have a very early flight to catch in the morning, so I think I'm going to turn in. I'll need to be up by five."

"Our plane leaves at seven-thirty," Ryan explained to his mother, moving in closer to Kate. "I'm not ready to go to bed yet, but let me walk you up to your room."

"Okay," she said, looking up at Ryan with a playful grin. Then she turned her attention to his mom. "Thank you so much, Jeanie, for the dinner you laid out and for your hospitality."

"You're welcome. Good night, hon."

As Kate turned to walk toward the staircase, she called out to Ryan's dad, who was across the room starting to doze off in his easy chair. "Good night, Jack."

"Night," he moaned, with his eyes remaining closed.

"I'll be right back, Mom. I have something to tell you." Ryan escorted Kate upstairs to her room, where they paused at the door.

"What exactly are you planning to tell your mom?" she asked.

"About the break in the case. Why?" He thought for a moment. "You don't think I was going to tell her about us, do you?"

"I wasn't sure. It kind of sounded like it."

"She would definitely be pleased, but no, I meant I wanted to tell her about the lead," Ryan assured her. "I think we can keep this thing between us to ourselves, for just a little longer."

"So there is something between us?"

"I don't know exactly what yet, but I definitely hope so." He lingered for a moment, studying her face. Then he leaned in and gave her a short and sweet kiss good night. "I'd better let you get to bed. Good night." He opened the bedroom door for her and then headed toward the stairs.

"Okay, good night," she said as he walked away. "See you in the morning."

Strolling into the kitchen, Ryan found his mother perched on a stool at the center island, stirring sugar into her cup of tea. She looked up when he walked in and her eyes brightened.

"Well?" she asked, raising her eyebrows, obviously hoping for some juicy details about their budding romance.

"I just wanted to tell you and Dad that we got a phone call tonight from one of the detectives in Seattle, and they may have a lead in Kate's sister's disappearance."

"Oh." His mother sounded a little disappointed. "Don't get me wrong, I think that's really good news. I hope it pans out. But, well...I just thought you were going to tell me about something else."

"You mean something about me and Kate?"

"Yes," she admitted.

"Mom, you know a gentleman should never kiss and tell," he said with a wink, making his mom's face light up with a smile. "I have to be up early tomorrow too, so I think I better turn in as well. Night, Mom." Ryan leaned over and gave his mom a peck on the cheek.

"Night, Son."

Ryan's dad was fast asleep in his favorite chair, snoring.

~*~

"I'd better go and get some shut-eye, Sis. We have a big day tomorrow," Ethan said, a wicked smile spreading across his lips. He set his empty beer bottle down on the coffee table, stretching as he stood up from the sofa.

"What's the plan?" Suki questioned, getting up out of her chair and following him to the kitchen.

"The plan I had is mostly out the window. The idea is still to kill Kate, but the details keep changing. I hadn't planned on her running off to Idaho. Now I'll have to rethink the timing of things."

"I don't want to fly by the seat of my pants," Suki moaned, "not on something this important."

"I get it," he said, scratching his neck then running his hand over his face. "But we don't know exactly when she'll be back in Seattle. You call me when you hear from her, and we'll firm up the plan." He seemed a little jittery and anxious to leave.

"So what are you thinking?" she pressed. Suki could tell by his restlessness that her brother needed more drugs, which was not good. She needed him to be clearheaded if they were going to get away with his plan.

"I'm gonna grab her and take her somewhere secluded, and I'm gonna make sure she knows who I am and why I'm doing this. She's got to know!"

"Are you on something?" Suki already knew he was—she just wanted him to know she knew.

"I'm okay—get off my back!" Ethan hollered. "I...I just need a little something to calm my nerves, that's all."

"You need to be sober and focused tomorrow," Suki ordered, grabbing hold of one of his arms.

"I will be," he said, shaking loose from her grip.

"Do you have a gun?"

"No. I could get my hands on one easy enough if I need to, but I'd rather use my knife, the one Dad gave me." He pulled a switchblade out of his back pocket and clicked it open. "I thought that would bring things around full circle, ya know? I could slit her throat, or stab her maybe," he said, his eyes focused on the blade as he brandished the knife. "Less noise, you know. I don't want anyone calling the cops 'cause they heard gun shots."

"You didn't take that thing with you to L.A., did you?" Suki asked.

"Nah, I left it at my place here. Those airport guys would've snatched it from me for sure."

"I just know you keep it on you most of the time."

"Yeah, I do, but give me some credit, Suki. I'm not stupid."

"Okay, okay. So, how are you planning to grab Kate?"

"I'm thinking on it, little sister. I have some thoughts I'm kicking around, but I have to know when she's back and where she's at. That's why I need you to call me when you hear from her."

"All right. I understand," she assured him.

"I gotta go, Sis."

"And what about me? When are we going to connect and get out of here? The cops will be looking for us when Kate turns up missing too."

"I'll let you know as soon as she's dead, so have your bags ready, and pack lightly."

"Okay," Suki agreed. They moved from the kitchen toward the front door. "Are you going to need my car?"

"I don't think so. I can pick one up off the street. Can't have the police knowing what kind of car to be on the lookout for."

"I went to the bank today and withdrew all my savings, like you asked. I have about two thousand dollars, which isn't much," she told him. "How much do you have?"

"I have a few thousand. You don't have to worry, I'll take care of you."

"From your drug sales?" Suki frowned. He had gone to jail once already, and she hated that he went right back to it when he got out.

"Money is money."

"I guess," she responded, knowing any further discussion about the subject was futile. "Is that going to be enough, though?" she asked, worry lines once more creasing her forehead. Her savings and his drug money did not seem like enough to keep them very long.

"It will be for now. You just do what I told you to tomorrow, and it'll all work out."

"Well, I don't work tomorrow, but I will need to go check on Whitney again, give her some more sleeping pills."

"Yeah, we don't want her dying on us just yet." Ethan put his ball cap and jacket on, preparing to go back out into the rainy night. He was staying a few blocks away at his usual place, a cheap hotel. "I really gotta go."

Suki opened the apartment door for him and looked up into his cold, dark eyes. She could see he was bent on killing Kate regardless of the cost to her sister.

"G'night, Sis," Ethan said as he slipped out the door.

"Night."

After locking the door, Suki went in the kitchen to put the tea kettle on to boil. She picked up Ethan's beer bottles, strewn about the living room, and tossed them in the trash as the doorbell sounded. She looked through the peephole, thinking her brother was back for something he'd forgotten, but she was wrong. She saw it was the two police detectives, instead. *Did they pass Ethan in the hall?*

Pulling in a quick breath, she unlocked the door and opened it. "Yes, can I help you?" she asked, trying to keep her nerves under control.

"Sorry to bother you so late, ma'am, but can we come in for just a moment?" Detective Porter requested.

"Sure, I guess." Suki stepped aside and let them in. "What's happened? Did you find Whitney?" she asked, trying to sound hopeful.

"No, not yet, but we have a photo we think might be a clue. Can you identify the people in this picture?" Will held the photo up for her to take a look.

She looked at it for a few moments, realizing it was a picture of her and Ethan, taken several years ago. Her hair was a dull medium brown back then, and she carried a few more pounds. Ethan's hair was cut short and neat, not the unruly mess he often hid under his hat these days. Her heart began to thump hard, and some of the color drained from her face, struggling not to give herself away.

"No, I don't think I know those people. Who are they?" she asked innocently, thankful it wasn't a close-up of them.

"Well, that's what we're trying to find out."

"Oh, silly me. Of course, that's why you're here. I don't know what I was thinking," she said, putting on her best airhead impression. The kettle began to whistle in the background. "Would you guys like some tea?"

"No, thank you, it's late. Sorry to have bothered you, Miss Gorman," Patel apologized.

"No bother. I want to help. Sorry I couldn't identify them," she remarked as she opened the door to let them out. "Good night."

That was close, she thought to herself, as she turned the dead bolt. *We'd better move fast once Kate is back, before someone does identify us in that photo and starts putting things together.*

CHAPTER 11

HORIZON FLIGHT 2269 was on final approach to SEA-TAC. Kate and Ryan had gotten to the airport before sunrise and were arriving in Seattle as the early morning sun was beginning to break, casting an orange glow at the horizon.

During the flight, Kate had been studying the photo on Ryan's phone, trying to make out the faces, but no matter how long she stared at the picture, it was not big enough or sharp enough to identify the people in it.

Grabbing their carry-on bags as they left, they got off the plane as fast as they could. After making a quick sprint to the parking garage, they were soon on the freeway and headed to the police station. Kate called Detective Patel to let him know their plane had landed and they were on their way to meet him.

"Porter and I are both here sifting through the computer files once more. I'm sorry to say we haven't found anything new. Hopefully, you'll be able to identify the people in the photograph, and it'll give us some direction in this investigation."

"I hope so, too. We should be there in about twenty minutes," Kate said, before hanging up.

She caught Ryan glancing at her while he drove. "Raj and Will are already at the office waiting for us," she told him.

Wrapping her arms around herself, she let out a sigh. "Whitney's running out of time, isn't she?"

"Now, let's stay positive, Kate. We don't know anything yet. This photo might be nothing. But, on the other hand, it might be a clue that busts this whole case wide open and leads us to finding your sister."

"You're right, but..."

"But nothing. We'll be at the station in just a few minutes, and then you can get a good look at the picture."

Kate wanted Ryan to be right. This photograph could be the key to figuring out what happened to Whitney and where she was. She didn't want to think of the alternative.

"I wonder if Suki would know who the people in the photo are," Kate said.

"That's a thought. Let's ask Raj and Will when we get there."

"Ugh! I wish I had thought of that last night. They could have gone right over to the apartment and shown it to her. Then Whitney may have been found by now."

"Don't beat yourself up about it. We'll ask them in just a few minutes."

"What a great sister I am. I was so wrapped up in what was going on between you and me last night that it never even occurred to me." She whipped out her phone again and began dialing.

"Who are you calling?" Ryan asked.

"Detective Porter." The phone started to ring and Will picked up.

"Kate? I thought you were on your way in?"

"We are, but I was wondering if you thought we should ask Suki if she could identify the people in the photo."

"Yes, we went over to her apartment last night and showed her the photo, but she said she didn't recognize them."

"Oh, okay then. That's all I was calling about. I guess we'll see you in a few minutes." Kate hung up and told Ryan what Porter had said.

"See, they're on top of it. It's their job to think of these things, not yours. Don't be so hard on yourself."

"You're right. I'm just so anxious to find her. Can't you go any faster?"

~*~

Ryan held the door open and Kate dashed into the police station first, heading directly back to the squad room. Patel and Porter were waiting for them, and a print out of the photo lay on the desk.

"Good morning, Kate, Ryan," Raj said.

"Good morning," Ryan replied.

"Is this the photo?" Kate asked as she picked it up. "Sorry, good morning. I don't mean to be rude, I'm just so anxious to see the picture." She held it up and studied the faces for a moment. Then her eyes narrowed and her head cocked slightly to one side.

"Oh, my gosh," she whispered under her breath.

"What?" Ryan asked.

"I know who these people are," Kate replied, glaring at their faces, stunned by the realization.

"You do?" Detective Porter asked, sounding encouraged that they finally had a lead. "Who are they?"

Kate swallowed hard before responding. A flood of memories rushed into her mind and her heart began to thud. She sat down at the desk, feeling weak in the knees.

"Are you all right?" Ryan asked.

She nodded yes.

"Who are these people?" Porter asked again.

She raised her gaze to him. "Suzanne Henderson and her brother, Ethan."

"How do you know them?" Patel inquired.

"It's been a long time since I've seen them. About ten years ago, I was in a car accident with their mother."

"Is the mother okay?" asked Porter.

"No." Kate paused, thinking back to that terrible day. "No, she died in the accident. As a matter of fact, it was ten years ago this month."

"That's too bad. I wonder, though, why would your sister write 'Suki & guy' on the sticky note and the file name?" Porter questioned.

"I don't know," Kate replied. She studied the photo again, concentrating on the faces. "She kind of looks like—"

"Looks like who?" Patel asked.

Kate's eyes narrowed as she focused on her face. "You know, I think the girl is..." Kate's eyes widened and she stopped breathing for a moment.

"Is who?" Ryan pressed.

"I think she's Suki! I think Suzanne Henderson is Suki Gorman."

"The roommate?" Patel asked.

"I thought there was something not quite right about that young woman," Porter mentioned. "I checked her out, but I didn't find anything. Probably because I had the wrong name."

"That's why Whitney wrote Suki on this picture file," Kate said. "She figured out Suki was Suzanne."

"Okay, but what about the guy?" Patel asked.

"Her brother, I guess. I don't know. I haven't seen her family since the accident."

"Why would Whitney question the photo? There was something about this photo that obviously made her suspicious," Porter mused, trying to think through Whitney's motivation.

"Oh, my gosh! Oh, my gosh!" Kate hollered as she suddenly put two and two together.

"What's the matter?" Ryan asked.

"There's a guy that I think has been following me," Kate said.

"The guy with the blue ball cap," Ryan recalled.

"Yes, I think this may be him."

"What? A fella's been following you? How come you never said anything to us?" Porter asked, putting both his hands on his hips. "This could be important!"

"I'm sorry, I wasn't sure," she apologized.

"What's his full name again?" Detective Porter asked in an irritated tone, grabbing a pen and pad off the desk to write it down.

"Ethan Henderson," she replied.

"We'll check him out, see what his story is. Anything else you haven't told us?" Porter questioned.

"No, I don't think so," Kate said.

"Why do you think Suki and her brother might want to hurt Whitney?" Patel asked.

"I don't know. I remember that at the time of the accident, their family blamed me for their mom's death. They were pretty angry, but that was a long time ago. Besides, I was the one driving, not Whitney. She was only fourteen then."

"Sounds like we need to bring Suki in for questioning," said Porter. "The press has been putting Whitney's photo out there, trying to help us find her. Maybe they can make a connection to Suki and Ethan if we put their photos out there, too."

"Can you do that?" Kate asked. "I mean, she's not a suspect yet, is she?"

"All we have to do is tell a couple of TV stations we're bringing someone in for questioning as a person of interest, and they'll be clamoring outside the station with cameras," Porter said. "We'll make a couple of calls and put the word out. We just need to find Suki first so the press is alerted as to when we're bringing her in."

"I don't think you should go back to the apartment until they have her in custody, Kate," Ryan warned.

She was glad he'd come to the police station with her. It gave her some comfort to hear him being so protective of her.

"I agree," said Porter. "Can you keep her with you, Ryan?"

"I think I can handle that," Ryan replied. "I just need to check in with my office and see what's going on there, and then I'm all hers."

"Do you think Suki is at home?" Patel asked Kate.

"I don't know. I haven't been there since yesterday. Let me give her a call and see," Kate offered.

"That'll work," Patel said.

Kate dialed Suki's number and listened to it ringing.

"Hello."

"Hey, Suki, this is Kate."

"Hi, Kate," Suki responded.

"I just wanted to let you know I'm back in town," Kate said, glancing up at Ryan.

"I've been wondering what happened. What did you find out in Boise? Was it Whitney?"

"No, fortunately, it wasn't her."

"Oh, I'm so glad to hear that."

"I'll be coming back to the apartment a little later. Are you there now?" Kate asked.

"No, I was just leaving to go by my work for a little while, but I'll be back this afternoon."

"Okay, I'll see you later, then," Kate said, trying not to give anything away. She hung up her phone and stuck it in her pocket. "Suki's on her way to work, she said."

"Where does she work?" Porter asked.

"The Underground Tour. You know, that place that shows where the original Seattle streets use to be."

"Oh, yeah, yeah, I know that place. I went there once," Patel said.

"We'll pick her up there," Porter decided. "I'd like to be waiting for her when she comes out, no sense trying to track her down in the maze of the underground city. When does she get off?"

"I don't think she's actually going to be working today. It sounded like she just had to stop by there for some reason, like picking up her paycheck or something."

"Maybe we can hurry and get there before she does. Then we can pick her up before she goes in," Patel suggested.

"That's a good idea," agreed Porter. "We'd better get going if she's already on her way."

"Do you want us to wait here for you?" Ryan asked as the two detectives headed for the door.

"No, we don't need you for now. You guys go do something for the rest of the day, away from the apartment, and we'll call you when we know anything," Detective Porter told them.

"Johnson!" Porter called to a young uniformed officer in the next room.

Officer Johnson sprinted into the squad room. "Yes, sir?"

"I need you to call the local TV stations and let their news directors know we're bringing in a person of interest in the Whitney McAllister disappearance. Tell them they have about twenty minutes to get their crew over here and set up. I want them already in place when we bring her in."

"Will do, sir." Office Johnson hurried back to his desk to jump on his assignment.

"Kate, Ryan, don't worry. We'll call you when we know something," Porter assured them. "Let's go, Raj."

~*~

Suki boarded the bus to Pioneer Square to check on Whitney one last time. Ethan assured her he would take care of Kate today. After that, they could get out of Seattle for good. She hoped she could find a way to let someone know where Whitney was, once she and her brother were safely out of the state.

She called her brother, as promised, when she knew for sure Kate was back in Seattle.

"Ethan, this is Suki. I just heard from Kate and she's back in the city."

"Did she say where she was?"

"No, but she said she'd meet me at the apartment later this afternoon."

"Where are you now?"

"I'm on a bus going to my work. I need to check on you-know-who," Suki told him, keeping her voice down and looking around to make sure no one was listening.

"Call me when you're on your way back to the apartment. I'll meet you there. We'll both be there when Kate comes back. I can take care of her then."

"I don't want to be there. I couldn't stand it."

"I'll take her back to Whitney's room. You won't have to watch."

"But, Ethan..."

"Hey! You said you wanted Kate to pay for what she did to Mom just as much as me. So stop your whining and let's get this over with. Then we'll grab our stuff and get out of this place."

"All right. I'll call you when I'm leaving to go back home."

The bus reached the Pioneer Square stop and Suki got off. It pulled away, leaving Suki standing on the sidewalk. She put her gray scarf over her head and scurried across the street to the Underground Tour building, approaching the main entrance. Her mind was set on what she had to do, hoping to sneak in and out undetected one last time. As she reached out to put her hand on the door handle, two men stepped up to her.

"Suki?" Detective Porter said, coming up to her on her right side.

She stopped cold, recognizing his voice. She looked up at him, then over to Detective Patel, who was now on her left.

"Hello, Detectives," she said, attempting to stay calm.

"We have more questions for you, so we'd like you to come with us," Porter said.

"I have to go to work right now. Can't I come down to the station and talk to you a little later?" Suki responded, trying to sound casual.

"I'm afraid not," Porter said, taking hold of her arm and leading her to the black unmarked police car they left parked at the curb just around the corner.

"But, you don't understand. I need to—"

"You need to what?" Porter cut her off in midsentence.

She couldn't explain to him what she needed to do without giving herself away. "Never mind," she relented. If they were only going to question her, she thought, she would be out of there in an hour or two and then she could check on Whitney.

Patel opened the door for her, helped her into the backseat, and then they whisked her away to the police station.

~*~

A frenzy of news reporters and TV cameras were waiting for them as they pulled up to the station. Parking in clear view of the cameras, Detective Patel pulled Suki out of the car. Both detectives escorted her at a snail's pace through the flurry of cameras and microphones and the volley of questions being thrown their way.

"Is this woman under arrest?" one reporter called out.

"Did she kidnap Whitney McAllister?" another shouted.

"Have you found Whitney's body?"

"Did this woman kill Whitney?"

The questions came in rapid fire, one building upon the other. As they approached the front door, the detectives turned and lingered for a few moments, letting the press get plenty of video and photos of Suki.

Once inside, Porter and Patel ushered her into one of the interrogation rooms and left her there alone, telling her they needed to go and gather the case file.

"Just cool your jets here and I'll be right back," Porter said, as he shut the door.

Sitting in the bare room, she nervously scratched her head, crossed her arms momentarily, then uncrossed them, spreading them out on the table. *What could they possibly have on me? And why did they need to bring me to the police station to ask me questions? They always came to the apartment before. Why the police station now.*

The fluorescent lights were glaring, putting a strain on Suki's eyes. The air in the room was warm and stuffy. She put her elbows on the table, propped her head on her hands, and closed her eyes to think.

Her thoughts went to Whitney, lying asleep on the filthy bed in total darkness. Without more sleeping pills, she'd eventually wake up. With her hands and feet tied to the bed and duct tape over her mouth, maybe she wouldn't be able to make much noise, Suki hoped. But, if she started jerking the brass bed around, she could make enough racket to possibly draw the attention of a tour passing by.

Oh, why did I let Ethan talk me into this? She leaned forward, stretched her hands straight out on the table, and laid her head down on them. *The police know something. They have to, or I wouldn't be here. And if I can't get back to the underground city to check on Whitney, she might give us away.*

And what's with all the press? They were snapping pictures and screaming out questions like I was being arrested or something. Oh, no! She sat up and buried her face in her hands. *What if I am arrested and I can't get out of here?*

Scenario after scenario flashed through Suki's mind and panic began to set in. For just an instant, she wanted to spill her guts and tell the cops everything—to save Whitney and save herself—but she soon pulled that thought back. She'd have to betray her brother, and there was no way she would do that. He wasn't much, but he was all she had left.

Taking a slow and deep calming breath, she glanced around the room, wondering when the detective would be back. She leaned back in her chair and closed her eyes to give them relief from the glare. *I'll wait*, she decided, *until I know what the police have. Maybe I'm making more of this than I need to.*

The door swung open and Detective Porter walked in. He dropped a manila folder down on the table with a *thud* and took a seat across the table from her.

"Sorry to take so long," he said, opening the folder and leafing through the papers. She watched him with interest but did not reply.

"Miss Gorman, I need to know where you were the night Whitney McAllister went missing."

"Me? Why, I was at home. I came home from work and Whitney wasn't there. I told you all of this before. It should be in that report."

"I want you to tell me again," Detective Porter said, "from the beginning."

"Whitney wasn't there when I got home from work Saturday evening, so I assumed she went out with friends or had a date. When I woke up the next morning, she still was not home. I waited all day for her to come home, but she didn't. I was worried. It wasn't like her to stay out all night. And then to stay out all the next day without letting me know, that *really* wasn't like her."

"Go on," Porter said.

"That's when I called her sister in L.A., you know, Kate. She said she would call the police to report Whitney missing, but then she didn't. She was told she couldn't file a report yet because she hadn't been missing for twenty-four hours. That's what she told me, anyway. It's all there in the report," she said, pointing at the folder.

Porter folded his hands on top of the file.

"Did I do something wrong?" Suki asked, shifting in her seat and crossing her arms in front of her. "You don't think I had anything to do with her disappearance, do you?"

"It's just routine, Miss Gorman. We have to ask everyone these questions, check everything out," Porter said, appearing to make a note on a page in the file.

Then, he pulled out the photo he had shown her the night before and spun it around with a couple of fingers so it faced her.

"And, I want to ask you to take another look at the photo I showed you last night," he said. "I thought maybe after you'd had some time to think about it something might have jogged your memory, and you could tell us who these people are." He paused and studied her face as if trying to read her reaction.

"Well, let me see." Suki picked up the photo and pretended to examine it, relieved that this was why they had brought her in. "No," she shook her head slightly, "I still don't know who these people are."

"Really?" Porter questioned, arching his eyebrows.

"I don't." Suki insisted.

"You, Miss Gorman, are a liar."

Suki's eyes widened at his accusation.

"Or should I say Miss Henderson?"

Her mouth dropped open.

"Isn't this you and your brother, Ethan?" he pressed.

"I'm not saying another word," she said as she crossed her arms again and looked toward the door, wishing she could get up and run out.

"Why would you lie about it if you didn't have anything to hide?"

Suki shook her head and looked down, refusing to answer.

"Tell me, did you or your brother have anything to do with the disappearance of Whitney McAllister?" he demanded.

Suki looked the detective in the eye and pressed her lips together hard. Bringing her right hand up to her mouth, she defiantly made a gesture like she was turning a key and locking her lips. Then she crossed her arms once more, sat back in her chair, and glared at him, unwilling to give up herself or her brother.

Porter continued to pepper her with more questions over the next hour, but she refused to answer any of them.

Finally, she spoke. "Are you arresting me?"

"Not just yet, however, we are going to hold you for a bit."

"You can't do that!"

"Actually, I could arrest you for lying to a police officer and obstructing our investigation, and I still might, but not yet. For now, I'm going to hold you for a few hours while we check out your story. Now, if you'd rather I arrest you and put you in the general prison population, I can do that."

Suki's pulse began to race and her face became flush. *What do I do? What do I do?*

Detective Porter crossed his arms and glared at her.

"Okay, you can hold me for a while, but I'm not answering any more questions. And I want a lawyer."

"Sure, I understand, but you need to know, Miss Henderson, if we find any evidence to indicate you had anything to do with Whitney McAllister's disappearance, you'll be charged with kidnapping. And if she's dead, you will be charged with first-degree murder. You might want to think about *that* while you're sitting in your cell."

Detective Porter slammed the folder shut and motioned toward the mirror.

Patel came in, took hold of Suki's arm, and escorted her out of the room. He handed her over to an officer with instructions to park her in a holding cell and call for a court-appointed attorney as soon as he could get around to it.

~*~

Suki sat alone in the jail cell wondering where her brother could be and how she was going to get out of police custody. Their plans appeared to be in real jeopardy.

Now, she only had two options, she thought. She could let Ethan carry out his plan and leave Seattle without her, or she could give her brother up to the police and both of them would end up in prison. Either way, she couldn't see any way that *she* was going to be set free once it all hit the fan. *Maybe this is the price I have to pay to avenge my parents' deaths.*

Before the police officer put her in the holding cell, he had confiscated all her possessions. Without her cell phone, she had no way to warn her brother that the police were onto them. *Maybe they'll find him, but it won't be because of me.*

CHAPTER 12

WHILE THE DETECTIVES were picking up Suki and questioning her, Ryan did his best to keep Kate distracted and out of harm's way. On the flight back to Seattle, she had mentioned to him that she hadn't been down to the Waterfront for quite awhile, so he suggested they go down there as a pleasant diversion. They grabbed a cup of clam chowder at Ivar's and sat out on the deck overlooking Puget Sound.

"The breeze coming off the water is a little chilly," Kate commented as she zipped up her jacket, "but the salty ocean air is refreshing. It's so nice not to have the rain for a change."

"I couldn't agree more," Ryan said.

"And this hot soup feels warm and comforting going down. It brings back memories of growing up here." She took another spoonful of her steaming chowder.

"Good memories, I hope."

"Yes, good memories," she replied, nodding. "I appreciate you keeping me company this afternoon," she told him, patting his knee. "You probably have work you should be doing, though."

"I'm happy to be here with you. My partner and my assistant are taking care of things." Ryan smiled at her, watching her long golden hair waving in the breeze. "I'll check in with my assistant later."

"Mmmm...I'd forgotten how good Ivar's clam chowder is. It's been years since I've been to this place."

"Me, too. Even though I live here, I'm so busy working that I don't take the time to come down here and just enjoy the Waterfront."

"I miss it," Kate said, with a tinge of sadness in her voice.

"Have you ever thought of moving back?" he asked, with something that resembled hope in his eyes.

"No," she replied, shaking her head and looking out over the water. "I left after my parents were killed. Since then, my sister has always come to Los Angeles to visit me. I never wanted to come back here to visit her. It was too hard."

Kate's countenance fell and her eyes began to water. "Maybe if I had stayed in Seattle my sister wouldn't be missing."

"You can't blame yourself for this. And you can't live your life based on *what ifs*." Ryan's attempt at comforting her fell on deaf ears.

"I should have stayed and been the big sister she needed."

"Don't do that to yourself. You don't know that."

Kate looked down at her watch again. "I wonder what's happening at the police station. I think I should call the detectives and see if they found anything out yet," she said, as she pulled her cell phone out of her pocket.

"Kate," Ryan placed his hand on top of hers as it held her phone. "It's only been about an hour since we left the station. Give them some time. They'll call you when they know something. They promised."

"I know, I know—but I can't stand the waiting. Where is my sister? I need to know if she's okay, Ryan." A couple of tears trickled down her cheeks, and the sea breeze turned them cold. She wiped them away with her hand, pulled her collar tighter around her neck, and crossed her arms against the chill.

Ryan scooted his chair closer to hers and put his arm around her. She leaned her head against his chest, relaxing in the strength and comfort it offered.

"It's going to be okay, Kate. Will Porter is a good detective. He's had a lot of years doing this. They'll find her," Ryan said. He kissed her temple and she snuggled closer.

"What about Raj? Isn't he a good one, too?" she asked.

"He's new to it, but Will is teaching him all he knows. Between the two of them, they'll figure it out."

"Look at me, blubbering like a baby," she said as she blotted a few stray tears with her napkin. "I like to pride myself on being a strong woman, but I've never had to deal with anything like this before. The not knowing is excruciating." She was glad they were alone out on the deck, for she would be embarrassed if anyone else was around to see her cry.

"It's okay, Kate, you're in a safe place. You don't always have to be so tough."

"Oh, but I do. Even though it was horrible for me losing my mom and dad, I had to be strong for Whitney," she went on. "It wasn't until I felt she was back on her feet that I took care of my needs and moved away. But now, if I lose Whitney, I've got no family left."

Ryan gave her shoulders a light squeeze and kissed her temple again.

"I've had to take care of myself in L.A.—support myself, protect myself, do *everything* for myself."

"Maybe this isn't the right time to ask, but, I've been wondering—"

"Wondering about what?" Kate asked.

"Well, we started to talk about it the other night at Kerry Park."

"What?"

"I've been wondering why you're alone in L.A., why no lucky man has swept you off your feet and married you yet."

A nervous laugh escaped her lips.

"Or is there someone back home waiting for you? You told me the other night you didn't want to talk about it, but ..."

"No, Ryan, there's no one waiting in L.A. for me."

"Why not?" he asked. "You're so, well, wonderful."

She chuckled again. "I appreciate you saying that, it's so sweet. I guess it's because I haven't had very good luck with men."

"At Kerry Park, you said there *was* someone. Care to elaborate?"

"All right, if you must know. I was dating a man for a couple of years. We even talked about getting married."

"What happened? Why didn't you marry him?"

Her tone turned somber. "I found out he was cheating on me, and not just once. Apparently, he thought that by marrying me, he could have a stable relationship with someone who would warm his bed and share his life, and he could have a little extra on the side too whenever he felt like it. He broke my heart, and I haven't been in another serious relationship since."

"Oh, man. What a fool! Well, it was his loss. That's all I can say."

"Thank you. That was what my friends said at the time, too."

An awkward silence hung in the air for a moment, his arm still around her shoulders.

"Hey, what do you say we get out of this place?" he offered, lightening the mood.

"Well, okay. What do you suggest?" Kate lifted her head and wiped her nose.

"Let's see, over there are the antique shops," he said as he pointed toward the shops across the street, nestled below an elevated roadway, "or there's the aquarium just down the street. I've heard good things about it. Or we could walk up the hill to Pike's Market and watch them sling the big fish around."

"Any of those sound fine," Kate replied. "You pick."

Just then, they heard the ferry's horn blow in Puget Sound and they both turned to look. "Or we could take the ferry over to Bainbridge Island," Ryan suggested. "I know a—"

"No, not Bainbridge Island," she said with an edgy sharpness in her voice. She sat up straight in her chair, and pulled away from him. "Remember? That's where I told you my folks died."

"I remember, but I thought maybe it would bring you some solace, like visiting a loved one's grave site."

"No, it wouldn't," she balked.

"Have you ever gone to the site of the accident?"

"Once, right after it happened, but I never want to go back."

"Maybe you need to. Sometimes it brings closure, visiting the place where their lives ended."

"It won't bring closure. It'll just reopen old wounds. Why are you pushing this?" Kate was getting agitated, and the refreshing cool breeze was now biting at her cheeks.

"Because it sounds like you've just been putting band-aids over a wound that's never fully healed, Kate. Maybe seeing where the accident happened again will help you heal."

Kate didn't want to go. How many times did she have to say it? She didn't want to dredge up the pain she had tried so hard to bury. However, several times she had told Ryan what a strong woman she was, so now she'd have to step up and prove it.

"All right, all right," she said, raising both hands in surrender. "Maybe it will help. I'll go, but if it gets to be too much for me, and I tell you we have to go, I need you to respect that and get us out of there. Will you do that for me?"

"Yes, I'll do that for you. I promise," Ryan said, crossing his heart with his finger.

She slipped her hand through Ryan's arm as they walked back to the parking lot. They climbed into his Land Rover and drove to the nearby ferry entrance. The ferry crewmen directed the long line of vehicles onto the ferry and the Land Rover came to a stop. Once parked, Kate and Ryan got out and climbed to the upper deck as the ferry travelled across the Sound to Bainbridge Island.

Among the other passengers on the deck, they found a place at the railing to watch the island draw closer. The nippy air coming off the water chilled them both. Ryan put his arms around Kate, and she slid her arms inside his coat, around his waist, and they clung to each other to keep warm. They could have gone inside and experienced the ferry ride from the comfort of the cushioned seating or from the inside of the Land Rover, but the unspoken intimacy of their warm embrace kept them on the cold deck.

Wrapped in his powerful arms, feeling the beat of his heart against her cheek, Kate closed her eyes and breathed in his masculine scent. The warmth of his body surrounding her made her feel safe and that somehow everything was going to be okay.

As the ferry approached the island, Ryan and Kate reluctantly let go of each other and made their way back down to the Land Rover. They waited inside the vehicle for the landing and for directions from the crew to disembark.

Kate's eyes darted back and forth from Ryan to the shoreline. She was sure that he could read the nervousness on her face as they drove off the ferry and onto the island.

"Do you remember where the accident happened?" he asked her.

"I think so. Just take the road to the right that goes to Poulsbo."

As they drove on the curvy road with forested areas on both sides, the scenery began to look familiar to Kate.

"There! I think that's the place," she exclaimed, motioning toward a huge tree across the road to the left.

Ryan pulled the vehicle over to the right shoulder and parked.

"It was a long time ago, but I remember that tree. See, the big cedar with the deep gash a couple of feet up from the ground?" she asked, pointing to it. "I think that's the tree my parents' car hit. I want to go see."

She unfastened her seat belt, opened the door, and slid out before Ryan had the chance to open the door for her. He climbed out, too, and they checked for oncoming cars before darting across the road.

They trudged through the underbrush about twenty feet, reaching the enormous tree. Kate crouched down to touch the damaged area where her parents' car had crashed into it. Tears flooded her eyes as she looked up at Ryan. A lump grew in her throat, and she could not find the words to express the anguish and sorrow that gripped her.

He put out his hand to help her up, and she gladly took hold of it. He pulled her to her feet and they backed away from the tree. She stood in silence, her emotions bouncing around inside of her like a metal ball in a pinball machine. It took all she had to contain herself and stand still, staring at the place where her mom and dad had died.

When she could no longer curb her tears, she began to weep. Ryan wrapped his arms around her, and she melted into him. He held her close and let her cry. The emotions she had stuffed down for so many years bubbled to the surface. The grief she had kept bottled up came spilling out. She was sure that he could feel the trembling and sobbing of her body against his.

When she was all cried out, Kate stepped back and Ryan let loose of his tender hold. Pulling a couple of napkins out of her pocket, she dried her face. Releasing a long sigh, she felt as if a huge weight had been lifted from her.

She turned back to look at the tree and remember where the lives of her parents had ended. That's when something caught her eye. She noticed there was a deep blue object hanging on an inside branch of a bush near the fateful tree.

"What's that?" she questioned, carefully stepping over the rocks and underbrush to reach the shrub, pulling a tattered baseball cap out of it.

"What is it?" Ryan asked.

She turned around and showed him the ball cap.

"It couldn't be," she said. "I'm sure it's just a coincidence."

"What do you mean?" Ryan asked.

"A dark blue baseball cap," she said, waving it back and forth.

"Like the one the guy who's been following you wears?"

"Yeah, Ethan, Suki's brother, but what are the chances?" She shook her head. "No, it's most likely nothing. There are thousands of blue ball caps."

"Do you think there's any chance he had something to do with your folks' accident?"

"I never thought so, but now, I don't know." She shrugged her shoulders. "On the other hand, what if this was his hat?"

"We might be able to find out, that is if there are any hairs or epithelia's still in it. Let's take it with us," Ryan suggested. "Maybe the police can run a DNA test and find out if it belonged to Ethan."

A chill slithered down Kate's back and she bristled. If Ethan had something to do with her parents' death, he might be behind Whitney's disappearance, too.

"It's probably nothing," she said, trying to shake the eerie cold feeling.

"Yeah, probably." Ryan nodded.

"Even though I fought you on it, I do appreciate you bringing me here," Kate said as she stepped in close to face Ryan, looking up into his gentle eyes. "If you hadn't, I would not have been able to let those feelings out. I had buried them so deep that I hardly knew they were still there."

"Then I'm glad we came." A twinkle lit up Ryan's eyes as the corners of his mouth turned up into a little smile.

She looked down at the baseball cap in her hand, then back up to him.

"While I know the chances are slim, if this ball cap ends up belonging to Ethan, this could be a big break in finding my sister. I wouldn't have found it without you." She pushed herself up on her tiptoes and planted a quick kiss on his lips. "Thank you."

"You're welcome, but how do you figure this ball cap can help find your sister?"

"It might mean Ethan is the one who took Whitney, if we can determine he was involved in the accident that killed my parents." Kate got more excited the more she thought about it.

"Be careful, Kate. Let's not get ahead of ourselves. We don't even know if this cap belongs to Ethan."

"I know, but it could."

"Yes, it could."

But with thousands of deep blue ball caps in Washington, the chances of this hat belonging to Ethan were remote. It was an odd coincidence, though.

"Why don't we head back to Seattle?" Ryan suggested. "We can call Will and Raj from the ferry."

"I wonder if it's safe for me to go back to the apartment yet," said Kate.

"We'll ask when we call."

She threaded her hand through the crook of his arm before they sprinted across the narrow highway and strolled back to the SUV.

~*~

Kate and Ryan decided to stop at a small coffee shop on the way back to the ferry to pick up a couple of warm drinks for the ride home. As they drove up to the order window, Kate leaned far over toward Ryan to get a better look at the menu on his side, her head leaning against his chest.

"Would you like to sit in my lap?" he joked.

"Sorry, it's just so hard to see the menu from my seat."

"Hello, can I help you?" asked the teenage girl who appeared in the window.

"I'd like a soy Chai latté, please," Kate ordered, craning her neck to read the choices.

"And you, sir?"

"A tall mocha cappuccino," Ryan replied.

Drinks in hand, within minutes they pulled into line to drive aboard the ferry returning to Seattle. Once on board and parked in place, Ryan turned off the engine, set his drink in the cup holder, and called Patel.

"Hey, Raj. This is Ryan. We're just checking in. I'm going to put you on speaker so Kate can hear, too." He clicked the speaker button and held the phone between them.

"Hi, Kate," came Raj's greeting.

"Hello."

"Where are you?"

"We're on the ferry on our way back from Bainbridge Island. Is there anything we should know?"

"Yes, as a matter of fact. We have Suki in custody," Raj said. "She's not talking, though. So she's in a holding cell for now."

"Do you think you'll be able get anywhere with her?" Ryan asked.

"Well, we made sure we had a bunch of reporters and camera crews at the police station waiting for us when we brought her in. We're hoping someone will recognize her when they plaster her face all over the news."

"That's a great idea," Kate said.

"Hey, did you just say you went to Bainbridge Island?" Raj asked.

"Yep, that's what I said." Ryan replied. "We had an afternoon to kill, so we hopped on the ferry."

"Why Bainbridge Island?"

"Kate and I went to visit the place where her folks died in an auto accident a couple of years ago. The funny thing

154

is, though, while we were there we found a navy blue baseball cap at the crash site, just like the one Suki's brother has been wearing every time we've seen him."

"Hey, this is Mariner baseball country, man. There are tens of thousands of people wearing dark blue baseball caps around here," Raj remarked.

"True, but this hat doesn't have a Mariner's logo on it. Do you think you could convince the guys to have it tested for DNA to see if he was there? 'Cause if he was, then maybe he was responsible for the accident," Ryan said.

"And that would mean it wasn't an accident after all," Kate added.

"Do you really think that's a possibility?" the detective asked.

"Well, think about it. If Suki and her brother are responsible for Whitney's disappearance, which might somehow be related to them blaming Kate for their mother's death, don't you think it might be a possibility?"

"Sure, it might be. I guess it couldn't hurt to have it tested. However, I'll have to check with Will since it's a closed case and was ruled an accident. Bring it in and I'll find out."

"Also, we wanted to ask if you think it's safe for Kate to go back to the apartment now?" Ryan looked over at her and caught her gaze.

"I don't see why not. We have Suki here in custody, and we will for quite a while, but I think you better stay close to Kate in case the brother shows up."

"All right. We'll come by with the ball cap before we head over to Whitney's place."

"See you then," Raj said.

Ryan hung up the phone, and reached for his cup of coffee. "Why don't we get out and stretch our legs?" he suggested, taking a sip.

"Sure. I wouldn't mind a stroll around the ferry."

Walking past a set of restrooms, Kate told Ryan she needed to use the facilities.

"I'll stay out here," he said. "I need to check in with my office anyway."

As Kate was in the ladies room, washing her hands at the sink, she couldn't help but wonder about Whitney. *How close are the police to finding my sister? Will they rescue her in time? Or is my sister even still alive?*

"Where are you, Whitney?" she whispered, as she dried her hands and looked at her own reflection in the mirror. "If Ethan killed Mom and Dad, he might also kill you."

He might also kill you. The words reverberated in her head. In that moment, as she looked into her own face in the mirror, staring into her own eyes, she suddenly realized she should be talking to herself and not Whitney. *He might also kill you.* Like a flash of lightning, the thoughts came to her. Perhaps Ethan was killing the people Kate loved and then he would kill her. Maybe this *was* payback for his mother's death—that he had been methodically plotting revenge against her for the past ten years. A frosty chill ran up her spine, and she shuddered with goose bumps.

Ryan was leaning against a steel pillar when Kate came out, and he stood up straight when he saw her. She must have been wearing a serious, worried look on her face, as if someone had delivered grave news to her in the restroom.

"What is it? What's wrong? Did you get a phone call?" Ryan peppered her with questions.

"No, no phone call," she answered somberly. "Just an epiphany."

"What do you mean?"

"This might sound weird, but while I was drying my hands I looked at myself in the mirror, thinking about Whitney. All of a sudden, it hit me—maybe Whitney's disappearance is more about me than her."

"I don't understand."

"It occurred to me that if Ethan caused my parents' accident, and if he's involved in Whitney's disappearance, it has to be because he blames me for his mother's death." The thought of it made her sick to her stomach.

"Oh, Kate, no."

"Could it be that he's taking the people I love the most before he comes for me?" She looked up at Ryan, searching his face for confirmation of her bizarre leap. "Or am I just crazy?"

Ryan looked unsure how to respond. She couldn't blame him. Anything was possible, but that was a pretty big leap.

"Let's not jump to conclusions," he said, taking her hand. "That would take a pretty twisted person."

"But is it possible?"

"Yes, I guess it's possible, but we don't have anything concrete that points to that. Let's try to be patient, wait to see what the police can get out of Suki."

"You're probably right." She swallowed hard, trying to keep a level head.

"When we get back to Seattle, we'll take the hat to them. Then, we can swing by my place so I can change out of these clothes."

"All right," she agreed. "I'd like to go by the apartment so I can change too."

"After that, we'll grab a bite of dinner while we wait to hear something. We can check back in with Raj and Will, if they haven't called by then. How does that sound?"

"That sounds good." Her spirit brightened a bit at Ryan's encouragement and his take-charge attitude. "I guess I just needed a reality check. My imagination is working overtime."

She wanted to believe that's all it was—her imagination running wild—but she had heard of worse in the news. "Oh, I forgot to ask, Ryan, everything okay at your office?"

"My assistant said she has everything under control. Did I mention she managed to send Vanessa away in a huff yesterday?"

Kate bristled at the mention of Vanessa. "No, you didn't. I would like to have seen that." After seeing her in action at the restaurant the other night, she could imagine it was quite a sight.

"Well, at this point, I'm not giving that woman a second thought. We need to focus on finding Whitney— that's the most important thing right now." He put an arm around her shoulders and pressed his lips to her temple.

"I couldn't agree more."

The sensation of his warm lips against her skin calmed her. She was grateful not to be going through this ordeal alone, but she couldn't fully shake the feeling that she might be right about Ethan.

CHAPTER 13

AS THE AFTERNOON WAS winding down and the sun began to set, Ryan and Kate walked into the police station and found Patel waiting for them.

"Here's the cap, Detective," Kate said as she handed it over to him. "I know it's a long shot, but I just have this nagging feeling that it belongs to Ethan Henderson. If he had anything to do with my parents' deaths, I need to know."

Raj took the cap and looked over at Ryan, then back at Kate. "You know there's got to be thousands of these things out there."

"Yes, I do realize that, Detective. Ryan reminded me this is Mariner country, but if you look at it, you'll see it doesn't have any logo on it. The one Ethan wears doesn't either," Kate said.

"You have a point there. That does narrow it down some, but even at that..." Raj shrugged. "I still need to get approval to have it tested, and logo or not, it's still a long shot."

"I know, I know, but if you can rule it out, then I can move on from this nagging theory. Please?" Kate implored.

"Yeah, I'll see what I can do."

"I appreciate that," Kate said. "Now, to the other thing. I heard you have Suki here in a holding cell. Is that right?"

"Yes, except she's not talking," Raj replied.

"Can I talk to her?" she requested.

"That's not usually done," Raj told her. "Let me see what Porter thinks."

"I thought you were *partners*," she said.

"We are, but he's the senior partner. There could be implications, so I'd like to get his take on it. Why don't you guys come back to my desk?"

Ryan and Kate followed him to the squad room where they found Will Porter seated at his desk, on the telephone.

"Thanks for your help," he said to the person on the other end of the line. He stood as he hung up the receiver.

"Hey, Kate and Ryan, I'm glad you're here. We've gotten some good television coverage on Suki being brought in for questioning in Whitney's disappearance, and the tips are starting to come in."

"That's great news," Ryan said, glancing at Kate.

"Anything sound helpful?" she asked, her eyes lighting up with optimism.

"Not yet, but maybe soon. It depends how that last tip pans out. Now, I don't want to get your hopes up, and this is off the record, but the person on the other end of that phone call claimed she was Suki's foster mother when she was a teenager."

Porter looked down at his notes. "Said her name was Mrs. DiMarco and that she saw the story on TV showing Suki being brought in for questioning regarding Whitney's disappearance. She wants to talk."

"That's good, right?" Kate struggled to keep her feelings in check. The detective was right, she shouldn't get her hopes up yet.

"Maybe yes, maybe no. Can't say until we talk to the woman." Detective Porter seemed as if he might be regretting having said anything about the woman to Kate. "I think Ryan can vouch for the odds of a tip panning out."

"That's true, unfortunately," Ryan nodded.

"Detective, I was wondering if I might be able to talk to Suki myself. Maybe she would open up to me," Kate said.

Raj looked at Will, raising his eyebrows inquisitively at the suggestion.

"I'm sorry, Kate, I can't let you do that." Porter sounded adamant. "Suki has asked for an attorney, and I don't want to do anything that could be construed as trying to get information out of her without her lawyer present."

Kate was willing to try anything she could to find her sister, but Detective Porter reminded her there were rules and protocol—his hands were tied.

"Well, I thought I'd ask." Kate crossed her arms and rested her hips against his desk.

"Why don't you guys go and get some dinner, and we'll call you if we catch a break on any of these tips. Okay?" Patel suggested.

"That's a good idea." Ryan took her hand. "These detectives don't need us underfoot."

"All right," Kate said, "but you'll call us the minute you know something, won't you?"

"Yes, yes, absolutely. Now go, have dinner and try to relax. I promise we'll call you when we know something," Raj said.

~*~

"Hey, everyone gets a phone call. Where's mine?" Suki asked the female officer as she walked by the holding area.

"I thought you called a lawyer," the officer replied.

"No, I didn't. I mean, I asked for one, but I didn't call. I was told they'd be appointing one for me," Suki said. "So? Can I use the phone or what?"

"Fine. Come with me. Payphone's down the hall." The officer unlocked the cell and opened the door. "But you only get fifteen minutes, so make it count."

Suki was elated. They may have her cell phone, but at least now she could try to reach Ethan. The female officer gave her change for the phone and reminded her of the time limit before stepping a few feet away to wait.

She nervously dialed his cell number, hoping he would pick up.

"Hullo."

"Oh, my gosh, Ethan. I'm so glad you answered." She spoke rapidly, not wanting to waste any time.

"Hey, Sis," Ethan replied, "about time you called. I haven't heard from you in awhile and you weren't answering your cell. Listen, I came by the loft to see if you were here. I snuck in behind one of your neighbors."

"You found the key?"

"Yeah, I let myself into the apartment, wandered around looking for you. I thought you said you weren't working today."

"I'm not, but listen, Ethan—"

"You said you didn't want to be here, so I figured you'd be scared and hiding somewhere."

"That's not it, Ethan," Suki was starting to think he was on something, again. She could hear him slamming things around, it sounded like the kitchen cupboards.

"Hey, you got anything to eat? I'm hungry. What's in the fridge?"

"Ethan."

"Hey, Kate's phone number. I'm taking this."

"Yeah, fine, take it. I don't need it. But, Ethan—"

"Cool, apples. I'm taking one of these too, Sis. I got my switchblade. Gonna practice carving up this apple here before I use it on Kate."

She could hear a rustling sound and little grunts coming from Ethan. *What is he doing?* She pictured him in her kitchen, brandishing the knife in a swashbuckling fashion.

Suki glanced over at the officer waiting nearby. Ethan was clearly in his own little world and she was getting frustrated. She didn't have much time to warn him.

"Should I slit her throat? No, stab her in the chest! Yeah. That's what I want to do, Sis. Hey, I'm gonna go lie on your bed and wait for Kate in there—surprise her."

Then, Suki could hear him crunching an apple in his mouth, followed by the sound of the television. Probably TV Land, it sounded like an old sitcom playing in the background. She recognized the theme song...it was one they used to watch as a family, when they were kids. Ethan laughed and then there was a muffled sound.

Did he drop the phone? I've lost him. She assumed he was off somewhere in his drug-induced world, again, watching old reruns.

"Ethan!" she shouted with her hand cupped over the receiver to muffle the volume of her voice, but there was no response.

"Time's up," the officer said, coming over and clicking off the phone. "If you ask me that was a wasted phone call. You barely got a word in. Let's go. Back to holding."

Suki went reluctantly. Now she really was screwed. She'd wasted her one phone call and her brother still had no idea where she was.

CHAPTER 16

THE KEYS JANGLED as Ryan unlocked the door and let Kate into his condo.

"Make yourself at home. I'm just going to change." He ducked into his bedroom.

She stood in the middle of the large space, admiring the architecture and design. Kate appreciated the open loft concept. It had a very contemporary feel with clean, straight lines and tall windows overlooking the heart of the city. It was well decorated in a manly bachelor sort of way. Sleek brown leather furniture sat against creamy white walls, softened with reds and rust, which toned down the stainless steel accents.

The place reminded her of a photo shoot she did in Malibu for an architectural magazine—the same clean lines and voluminous space, earthy colors and natural elements. The style filled her with a sense of peace and calm.

A few dishes sat in his sink, a pair of brown loafers rested by the sofa, and one of Ryan's jackets lay on the back of a dining chair, which gave his place a lived-in feeling. *Not messy, just comfortable*.

"Is there any place in particular you'd like to go to tonight?" Ryan called out from the bedroom.

From where Kate stood, she could peer into part of the bedroom and see Ryan, bare from the waist up, looking into his closet, searching for something else to put on. The sight of this partially-naked man, his chiseled upper body exposed, made her heart skip a beat. Heat rose in her cheeks and flowed down through her body.

"Um, yes, well...that place we went to the other night, Yellowfin's, would be good. I thought the food was excellent." Kate stepped toward the wall of windows so Ryan wouldn't catch her watching him dress.

"Yes, I think that would be good, too," he said as he stepped up behind her, now fully clothed, and wrapped his arms around her waist. She let out a nervous giggle at his surprising nearness. The comfort of his arms filled her with warmth and she did not resist.

"What a stunning view," she said, looking out at the city lights, leaning her head back on his chest.

"Yes, stunning," he agreed. They stood together enjoying the view for a moment, feeling the same physical and emotional attraction they had experienced the evening before at his folks' place. Brushing her golden hair back with his hand, he gently kissed the side of her neck.

A tingle rushed through her from her neck to her toes. She turned around and looked up into his eyes. He caught her gaze for just a moment then lowered his face. His lips covered hers and she felt the passion from that kiss send her blood pulsing throughout her body.

"Oh, Ryan," she heard herself sigh. The intensity of the kiss overwhelmed her, leaving her intoxicated. Her head was spinning, and she wondered where this was going to lead.

"Kate—" he started to say, interrupted by the ring of his phone. Thoughts instantly flew to her sister, hoping the detectives were calling with some news.

Her body stiffened and she stepped back from Ryan as he whipped his phone out of his pocket, not taking the time to check the Caller ID first.

"Hello, this is Ryan." He paused, listening. "Oh. Vanessa." He frowned, pausing again.

"Actually, yes. I'm in the middle of something important. Can I call you back tomorrow?" Ryan said, looking at Kate, shaking his head as if to say *no, I won't.*

After a longer pause, Ryan rolled his eyes. "Oh, brother," he mumbled as he hung up the phone and shoved it back in his pocket.

His response to Vanessa made Kate grin.

"Sorry about that," he said, running a hand down her arm, taking her hand in his, kissing her fingers. "Where were we?"

"I thought that call was going to be the police with some news about Whitney." She looked down and shook her head, taking her hand back. "What kind of sister am I, thinking about myself at a time like this?" She walked over to the window, crossed her arms, and looked out at the sprawling view of the city. "Where are you, Whitney?"

Ryan stepped up behind her and put his arms around her once more, enveloping her in his strength and comfort. The moment was broken, but he seemed to understand. "They'll find her, Kate."

"It's so hard to just wait. I need to be doing something."

"Let's head over to the apartment so you can change, and then we'll get some dinner. Maybe by the time we're finished eating, the cops will have gotten something out of Suki."

"We can only hope."

~*~

Kate turned the key in the lock and the door to the apartment made a creaking sound as it opened. They had been conversing back and forth, but they stopped when they heard a noise coming from Suki's bedroom.

Kate looked at Ryan, frightened at the possibility she was there. "Do you hear that?"

He nodded.

"Suki?" Kate called out. There was no reply.

"We know the police are holding her, so why is the television on in her bedroom?" she said, keeping her voice down.

Ryan shrugged in response. He led Kate down the hallway to check.

"Suki?" he said, as they entered the bedroom. The bed was mussed, like someone had been laying on it, but there was no one there.

Kate reached down and flipped the TV off. "I guess she must have forgotten to turn it off before she left this morning. I didn't think the police had released her yet."

"I'm sure they would've called us if they decided to let her go," Ryan said.

Kate noticed a photo sitting on Suki's dresser. She picked it up and examined it. It was a photo of Suki and Ethan with their mom and dad, a long time ago.

"What's that?" Ryan asked.

"Looks like a photo of Suki and her family quite awhile ago, before the accident. They looked happy."

"So, her mom died in the car accident. That must've been hard." Ryan said.

"Yes, I'm sure it was," she said sadly, remembering the death of her own mother.

"What about the dad?"

"I don't know," she replied, "but if Suki ended up in foster care, it can't be good." She set the photo gently back down on the dresser and walked out of the room.

"While you change, I'm going to call Yellowfin's and get a reservation."

"Okay. I'll just be a minute," Kate replied as she walked into Whitney's room and shut the door.

~*~

Kate and Ryan left the apartment building and strolled down to Yellowfin's Seafood Grille. The light rain had stopped and the air was almost dry again. Ryan held the door open for Kate and followed her inside.

"We have reservations," he told the young Asian hostess. "Wilson, for two."

"Yes, right this way, Mr. Wilson." She plucked a couple of menus from the cabinet and led them to their table.

Kate slid into the booth.

Ryan took off his jacket and slipped in across from her. "Well, what shall we have tonight?" He picked up the menu and scanned over it. "The Mahi Mahi looks good."

Her phone began to ring and she was quick to answer it. "Hello, this is Kate."

"Kate," said an unfamiliar male voice, "be quiet and listen carefully. If you want to see Whitney alive, you'll do what I say."

"What?" she asked.

Ryan raised his eyes from the menu and looked over at her.

"This is Ethan Henderson and I have your sister. Act like I'm an old friend. If you don't play along with me, I will kill her."

"Oh, hello, Cynthia," Kate said. "Sorry, I couldn't hear you at first."

Ryan returned to reading the menu.

"I want you to tell your date you need to go and use the ladies room. Do you understand?"

"Yes, I'd be happy to help you when I get back in town."

"Come out the rear door of the restaurant, through the kitchen. I left a package in the alley with instructions on how to get your sister back."

"Yes, Cynthia. That would be fun."

"Come out to the alley alone, or I promise you I *will* kill your sister."

"Okay, no problem. I'll see you then." The line went dead, so Kate pretended to hang up.

"Who was that?" Ryan asked.

"A friend from Los Angeles. She wants to get together when I get back." Kate put her phone in her pocket and scooted out of the booth.

"Where are you going?"

"I have to use the ladies room. Why don't you order the Mahi Mahi for me?"

"All right," he replied, going back to studying the menu. "I can't make up my mind."

As Kate walked toward the ladies room, she pulled her cell phone out of her pocket, switched it to vibrate and stuck it in her bra. Then, she veered off from her path to the restroom and headed in the direction of the kitchen.

She was terrified going out into the back alley alone, certain she was walking into a trap, but she was willing to do whatever she had to do to save her sister's life. If she didn't comply with Ethan's instructions, she knew he would kill Whitney—if he hadn't already.

By hiding her phone in her bra, she hoped Ethan wouldn't find it, and someone else might be smart enough to think to track her by the cell phone's signal. All she had was that hope. Without it, she feared they would never find her or her sister. She had to take that chance.

Kate paused before the heavy, metal door, summoning the courage to face what she feared was on the other side. She pushed the weighty door open and walked out into the dark alley. It automatically swung shut as soon as she was clear of it.

Someone stepped out from behind the door. She noticed a shadow move as she heard a couple of quick footsteps. Before she could turn, she felt the pain of something hard crack against the back of her head. Kate fell forward on the gritty wet pavement and everything went black.

CHAPTER 15

RYAN BURST INTO THE POLICE STATION, frantic and out of breath. He caught sight of Raj heading into the conference room. "Raj!"

Patel turned to the sound of his name being called. "Ryan?"

"I need your help."

"What's wrong?"

"Kate's missing!" he said between gasps of air.

"What?"

"We were at Yellowfin's Seafood Grille having dinner. Then, Kate got a phone call. She said it was a friend in Los Angeles. After that, she excused herself to go to the restroom, but she never came back."

"How long has she been gone?"

"About thirty-five minutes," he said, looking at his watch. "I tried calling but they said you were unavailable, so I rushed over."

"What happened?"

"She'd been gone more than fifteen minutes, so I got worried and went looking for her. I had the hostess check in the ladies room, then we checked the kitchen. Some of the kitchen staff said they saw her walk through and go out the back door." Ryan was growing frantic, his mind thinking the worst.

"Did you check outside the back door?"

"Yes, we looked around but didn't see anything out of the ordinary. Raj, I'm so worried. Why would she leave without saying anything?"

"I don't know. Maybe that wasn't really a friend on the phone."

"Yeah, maybe."

"We're about to question the foster mother. I think we may have caught a break."

"What about Kate?"

"I'll have a forensic team go over to the alley and investigate."

Just then, an officer ushered a middle-aged woman toward the interrogation room. Porter came out to greet her. He waved Raj over. "Patel."

"Listen, Ryan, I gotta go. Can you sit tight while we conduct this interview?"

"Is that her? The foster mother? Can I sit in?"

"Ryan—"

"I know what you're going to say. But technically, I'm not just any civilian."

Raj didn't look like he was going to budge.

"You got five bucks?" Ryan asked.

"Huh?" Raj appeared even more confused now, but Ryan stuck his hand out and nodded at him to come up with the five dollars. The detective reached into his pocket, pulled out the cash, and handed it to over.

Ryan shoved it in his pocket. "Okay, you just hired me as a consultant. Former cops do that all the time, right?"

"Well..."

"Patel!" Porter urged from the interrogation room door.

"Fine," Raj gave in, "but keep your mouth shut. Got it?"

Ryan nodded his head and followed his friend into the room.

Porter raised his eyebrows when Ryan entered, but Raj shrugged. "All right then." He seemed to understand Ryan's desperation. "Let's go sit down, shall we?"

"Ma'am," Detective Porter gestured to the short, round Italian woman to a chair at one end of the table.

She politely complied and took a seat. Patel followed suit, then Ryan. Once they were all seated around the table, Raj leaned in and whispered something to his partner. Ryan figured he was telling him about Kate. Porter whispered something back and then made the introductions.

When he got to Ryan, he seemed unsure what to say, so Patel jumped in, "Mr. Wilson is...a special consultant on the case, Ma'am."

That answer seemed to work. Porter nodded his agreement, then set down the case file, folding his hands on top of it.

"Thank you for coming in, Mrs. DiMarco," Porter started. Then he turned to Raj. "Detective Patel will be right back. He has to go arrange for a CSI team."

Raj got up and excused himself.

Porter turned back to Mrs. DiMarco. "Now, where were we?"

"I hope I'm not too late. Oh, that poor missing girl." She glanced down briefly at her hands clasped in her lap and shook her head. The pudgy, middle-aged woman looked like she'd had a hard life, with her wrinkled face, unruly curly black hair, and her ill-fitting clothes. Her concern for both Suki and Whitney sounded genuine.

"What did you want to tell us?" Porter asked.

"I don't know if you know the whole story," she began, looking at Ryan and Detective Porter.

"Why don't you start from the beginning and tell us everything you know about Suzanne."

"All right, from the beginning," the woman said. "When Suki was fourteen, which is what we called her, her mother was tragically killed in an auto accident—poor thing. After that, her father had started drinking heavily. I guess he had a really hard time with his wife's death. Because he drank so much, he ended up losing his job. Then there was her brother, Ethan, who was in college at the time. With his mom gone and his dad being fired, he had to drop out of school and come home. Eventually, according to what Suki had told me, they lost their big house and moved into a crummy little apartment. It was such a sad thing."

"Go on," Detective Porter said, just as Patel re-entered the room, nodding at his partner.

"Things just went from bad to worse," she said. "I guess the dad couldn't take it anymore, and he ended up killing himself. His son found him shot in the head in his bedroom—the dad's bedroom, that is. That's when Suki came to live with us as a foster child. Ethan was old enough to be on his own, but Suki was only fifteen."

"Have Suki and Ethan stayed in contact all these years?" Patel asked.

"Off and on. While Suki was with us, they did. He got into drugs and alcohol pretty bad. He would call or stop by occasionally at first, but if he was high, my husband would run him off. After awhile he quit coming around, and I don't know what happened after Suki turned eighteen and left us. That was the last we saw of her."

"I understand what you're saying, Mrs. DiMarco, that the family fell apart and the kids' lives were turned upside down, but can you tell us why you think Suki and Ethan would kidnap Whitney?" Porter asked.

"Because they blamed her sister, Kate, for their mother's death, of course."

Ryan leaned in closer when she said that. *Kate was right. Please be okay, Kate, please.* As much as this information was confirmation, he felt he should be out looking for Kate, not cooped up in this little room. But since he had promised Raj he wouldn't say anything, he sat back again.

"What do you mean?" Patel asked.

"Well, I overheard them a number of times talking about how all their troubles were Kate's fault. As you can imagine, the accident started everything going downhill. Losing their mom is what caused all the other horrible things that happened to that poor family."

"I don't understand, though, if they blamed Kate, why wouldn't they have kidnapped her instead of her sister?" Detective Porter questioned.

"I don't know. I just thought it had to be too big of a coincidence that Kate's sister was missing and you were questioning Suki. That's why I called you."

"Was Kate responsible for Mrs. Henderson's death?" Patel asked.

"I wasn't around them when it happened. I only heard Suki and Ethan going on and on about Kate McAllister and how it was all her fault. So, yes, I thought so, at first," Mrs. DiMarco explained.

"At first?" asked Patel. "What do you mean, *at first?*"

"I mean because that's all I heard. But later, after Ethan stopped coming around, I got something in the mail from the police department. It was a copy of Mr. Henderson's suicide note and a letter from a police investigator explaining they'd found the note in the police files and thought his children should have it."

"What did it say?" Porter asked.

"I have it right here." Mrs. DiMarco pulled the letter out of her purse, unfolded it on the table, and read it out loud. "Ethan and Suzanne, I can't stand the guilt and pain anymore. I have to put an end to it. I'm ashamed to admit it, but I had an affair and Mom found out the afternoon she died. She had been drinking when I came home and she confronted me. We had a huge fight and she ran out the door and drove off. I'm sorry I didn't stop her. *She* ran that stop sign when she was hit by the SUV and died. It was all my fault. Please forgive me. Dad."

"And you never gave this to Suki or Ethan?" Porter asked.

"No. At the time it came, Suki was starting to do better in school and make a few friends. Her brother had stopped coming around—I think he'd gotten himself arrested for drugs or something. I didn't want to stir things up again, so I just stuck it in a drawer and forgot about it. That is, until I saw Suki on the news today and heard them mention the name McAllister."

"This explains a lot," Porter said. "You've been a big help, Mrs. DiMarco."

"Thank you, Detective. I hoped I could be."

Ryan tried to process what this all meant. It seemed that Suki and Ethan had been plotting revenge, and it wasn't even Kate's fault. *We have to tell them. They need to know...before something happens to Kate!*

Then just before Ryan opened his mouth to say something, Porter said it for him. "Would you mind telling Suki what you just told us?" Porter asked. "I think she'll be more likely to believe it coming from you."

"Sure, if you think it would help."

"I do," he replied.

Porter stood up to leave. "Mrs. DiMarco, if you'll just wait here, I'll be right back with Suki."

She nodded her head in agreement and sat fidgeting with the note while Patel jotted down something in the case file.

Ryan sat in silence, trying to appear calm on the surface but inside he was struggling with doing nothing to find Kate. He reminded himself that if they could convince Suki she had been wrong then maybe she could reach Ethan—before he did something drastic.

Just then, Porter pushed the door open and ushered Suki in. She stopped in her tracks when she saw Mrs. DiMarco.

"Have a seat over there," Porter directed Suki, motioning toward the chair across the table from her foster mother. Suki did as she was told and sat down.

"Why's she here?" Suki asked Detective Porter, staring at her former foster mother with suspicion written all over her face.

"She has something she wants to tell you. So, we're going to leave you two to talk."

Suki turned quickly and shot Porter a questioning glance. "Where's my lawyer? I asked for a lawyer. I'm not saying anything without my lawyer!"

"Mrs. DiMarco isn't here to ask you any questions," Porter replied. "She wants to tell you something—something important. So sit still and listen."

He motioned to the door, and then Ryan and his partner followed him out. They stepped into the observation room next door, and they watched as Mrs. DiMarco explained the letter, handing it to Suki.

Then Porter turned to Ryan. "Raj tells me that Kate is missing. What happened? "

"We were at a restaurant and she got a call, then she told me she was going to the ladies room—but she never came back."

"Let's hope Suki spills her guts once she knows Kate is not responsible for her mother's death, and we can solve this case." Porter sounded exasperated.

Ryan looked toward the two women in the other room. "I hope she can tell us something."

"Well, let's go see what Suki has to say about Kate's disappearance," Porter said. They left the darkened room and burst into the conference room. Both women looked up as the men entered.

"Did you tell her yet?" Patel asked Mrs. DiMarco.

"Tell me what?" Suki questioned.

"Did you tell her Kate was not responsible for her mother's death?"

"I was just getting to that, Detective. You busted in here before she could finish reading the letter." The woman sounded irritated that they hadn't given her more time to talk to Suki.

"I'm sorry, but time is running out," Patel responded.

Suki looked from Ryan and the detectives to her foster mother. "What do you mean Kate's not responsible? Of course, she's responsible. She hit my mom's little compact with her big fat SUV when she ran the stop sign."

"No, honey. It was your mom that ran the stop sign. She'd been drinking and she'd had a fight with your dad. Read it," Mrs. DiMarco said, "it's all there in your dad's note."

They all sat in restrained silence as Suki finished reading the suicide note, anxious for her to be done. When she was through, she buried her face in her hands and began to weep, her red curls falling forward. She seemed to realize that all the hate and bitterness that she and her brother had harbored against Kate, all the revenge they had planned, was based on a misunderstanding.

Detective Porter's gaze moved from Mrs. DiMarco to Ryan and Patel. "Suki, please, where is Whitney?" he pleaded in a calm, even voice.

Mrs. DiMarco handed Suki a tissue from her purse, and the young woman wiped her eyes.

"How do I know this isn't a trick?" Suki asked. "Maybe this is a ploy to get me to talk." She raised her head a bit and looked at the men. "You could have found my foster mother and given her this note and told her to lie to me so I would talk."

"Suki, no," Mrs. DiMarco said, stretching her hand out across the table. "I wouldn't do that to you. Look at the handwriting. I think you know it's your dad's."

"Where is Whitney?" Porter asked again.

"And Kate?" Ryan demanded.

"Kate?" Suki prickled at the question. "How would I know? I don't understand. What do you mean *where's Kate?*"

"Kate's gone missing, too. You're telling us you don't know anything about that?" Patel questioned, placing his hands on the table as he leaned toward her. "I find that hard to believe!"

"Well, I—I—" Suki stammered.

She's hiding something, Ryan thought. *She may not know where Kate is, but she must know that her brother has taken her and what his intentions are. The question is, will she give up him up to the police?*

"Where's Kate? Spit it out!" Patel snarled.

"I don't know where Kate is!"

"But you do know who took her, don't you?" Patel pushed. "Now, come on, Suki, when you thought Kate was responsible for killing your mother, maybe you were willing to help Ethan. But now..." he paused, looked her straight in the eyes, "...how can you let your brother kill an innocent woman?"

Suki remained silent.

Ryan couldn't take his own silence any longer. "If you can let Ethan know about the note, and that it wasn't Kate's fault after all, maybe you could stop him before he goes through with his plans."

Raj shot him a warning glance and Ryan thinned his lips, forcing himself to stay out of it. He stepped back.

"Do you have any idea what he's done with her?" Porter asked, maintaining more composure than his partner or Ryan.

The young woman sat stony silent.

"Suki, for heaven's sake, tell them what you know," Mrs. DiMarco pleaded.

"I want my lawyer. I told you that before."

"If we have to wait for your Public Defender to show up," Patel said, "Whitney and Kate could be dead. Is that what you want?"

"No, but I need someone on my side to help me out of this," Suki replied.

"I understand, Miss Henderson, but look at it this way. Right now, you're in a little hole. It won't be so hard to dig your way out of it," Porter said. "However, if Whitney or Kate are found dead, you're going to be in a hole so deep you'll never see the light of day again—your brother, too. Now, tell me, do you still want to wait for a lawyer?"

Suki looked at Porter and paused, likely weighing her options. "No, I guess not, when you put it that way."

"Let me ask you again," Porter said, "do you know who took Kate?"

"I think my brother, Ethan, took her," she said, guardedly.

"Do you know where he would have taken her?" Porter questioned, leaning in closer to Suki, searching her eyes for the truth.

"No, I don't." Suki shook her head as she answered. "I wish I did, but, no."

"But you do know where Whitney is, don't you?" Patel asked.

"Yes," Suki hesitated, "but—"

"Tell us!" Patel yelled. "Where is Whitney McAllister?"

"Okay, okay, I'll tell you. She's in a hidden room in the underground city, below Pioneer Square, where I work," Suki cried, the truth spilling out. "I hid her in a locked storage room to get Kate to come to Seattle."

"Is she dead?" Porter asked.

"No, I don't think so," Suki replied, avoiding looking him in the eye. At least she seemed ashamed of what she had done to Whitney.

"You don't think so?" Patel questioned. The veins in his neck were visibly pulsating from the stress.

"I don't know, I don't know. I've kept her sedated with sleeping pills."

"Oh, Suki..." Mrs. DiMarco sounded stunned.

"I was going to check on her when you picked me up outside of the Underground Tours," Suki explained. "I didn't just leave her there."

Porter directed Raj to call for an ambulance to meet them at the building in Pioneer Square where the Underground Tour begins, and he dashed out of the room to make that call.

Then Porter stepped out in the hallway for a moment and Ryan paced back and forth, desperate to find Kate too.

Porter returned with a uniformed policewoman. "Suki, we need you to help us figure out where your brother took Kate. And we need to find Whitney now—right now."

She looked up at him with understanding. "Okay."

Time was not Whitney's friend and Porter's face had grown gravely serious. "I think you already know that I'm going to have to arrest you, but don't make it any worse. I need you to show us, this minute, where you're keeping Whitney. Hopefully, she's still alive."

"I understand," Suki agreed. "I never intended to kill Whitney..." she let the words trail off.

"Officer Diaz, after you handcuff her and read her her rights, meet me at my car. I want both of you to go with us to find Whitney."

"Yes, sir," the officer answered.

"Mrs. DiMarco. Thank you for your help."

"I hope you get there in time."

"You and me both."

At that, Ryan rushed out of the room and dashed to Raj's desk. Patel was on the phone calling for an ambulance. He stood by as Raj then phoned a junior officer, directing him to contact the manager of the Underground Tour to meet them there too, ASAP, to unlock the place and turn on all the lights.

"Did you hear back from the forensic team yet?" Ryan asked. "Do you have some word on Kate?"

"No, not yet. But the investigators have been all over the area behind the restaurant and didn't find anything."

"When was that?" Ryan asked.

"I sent a couple of CSI's out there when I stepped out of the room, while Will was questioning the DiMarco woman."

"Raj, I need to find Kate!"

"*You* need to find Kate? Ryan, you're not on the force anymore. You can't be running all over town trying to do our job."

"I know I'm not a cop, but I can keep my eyes open. If you let me ride along, I promise I'll stay out of the way."

"We've got to go and find Whitney," Raj said as he headed toward the door.

Ryan reached out and tapped Raj's arm to stop him. "I understand about Whitney, but what about Kate? Maybe I should take my own car."

"We don't have any leads on Kate yet. We'll continue questioning Suki in the car on the way to find Whitney. Hopefully, we can get her to tell us something that will lead us to Kate, too. But in the meantime, I can't have you doing anything crazy. Do you hear me?"

"I hear you, but if Kate *is* right about Ethan killing her parents, it's more than possible he took her. And if that's the case, you know he won't hesitate to kill her."

"We don't know for sure that he killed her folks."

"I know, but it's possible, isn't it?"

"I guess, anything's possible."

"So, let me come with you and Porter. I can help you question Suki."

"All right," Raj said, his eyes darting around to be sure no one was within earshot. He lowered his voice to almost a whisper. "You better stay in the car and wait, or we'll all be in a lot of hot water."

"You have my word."

"Raj!" Porter called out on his way out the door.

"I hope my partner agrees to this," Raj said. They sprinted to catch up to Porter and dashed out the door.

CHAPTER 16

Officer Diaz and Suki met them at Porter's car, and they all climbed in and sped off, lights flashing and siren blaring, to meet the ambulance and other officers at the Underground Tour. Ryan, Diaz and Suki rode in the back, while the detectives used the opportunity to try to draw more information out of their suspect.

"Suki, I appreciate the fact you decided to cooperate and show us where you've been keeping Whitney." Porter peered up to see her momentarily in the rearview mirror as he drove. "It was the right thing to do." He swung the car around a sharp corner. "But it's critical we find Kate, too. Do you have *any* idea where Ethan might have taken her?"

"Not really."

"What's he planning to do with her?" Patel asked, twisting in his seat to look at her.

Suki didn't respond. With her hands cuffed behind her back, she dropped her head down. A few tears fell onto her cotton blouse, leaving dark spots.

It took everything Ryan had not to reach over and make her talk.

"Suki, answer me," Patel pressed. He wore an expression that looked like he had the same bad feeling that Ryan had, when he saw her bending forward and crying.

"Suki, look at me! What is your brother planning to do with Kate?" he insisted. "Tell me."

She lifted her face. "He's going to kill her."

Porter glanced at the rearview mirror again, then over at his partner. Their eyes met with a look that said they didn't have much time.

"Think, Suki. You know your brother better than anyone else does. Where would he take her?" Porter demanded.

"I don't know!" she screamed, shaking her head from side to side. "I don't know. If I knew I would tell you!"

Ryan felt a thin layer of sweat forming on his forehead and his pulse began to race. He felt helpless as he sat beside Suki, listening to this unproductive line of questioning. If it were up to him, he would find a way to make her tell them what they needed. Suddenly his phone vibrated. He snatched it up hoping it might be Kate.

"Hello, Ryan," Vanessa said.

"This isn't a good time."

"But—"

"I can't talk now! Something terrible is going on—Kate is missing." He didn't want to discuss it with her, but he didn't want to get stuck talking to her either.

"Missing?" she asked. "Are you sure? I saw her not that long ago."

"You did? Where?"

"I was at Yellowfin's, on a date. When Jonathan and I first walked into the restaurant, I saw her head for the ladies room. It was weird—because all of a sudden, she turned and walked toward the kitchen instead."

"I was at the restaurant then. How come I didn't see you?"

"Because you had your head buried in the menu. I saw no reason to bother you."

"Vanessa, this is important. Did you see anything else?" Ryan asked. "Anything out of the ordinary?"

"As a matter of fact, yes, something peculiar."

"What?" Ryan pressed.

"I saw her stick her phone down her shirt, probably into her bra. I thought that was odd. Don't you think that was odd?"

"Yeah, that is strange," Ryan said, wondering why. "Anything else?"

"No, that was it. I just don't understand why you believe she's missing. It wasn't that long ago."

"I can't talk about it right now. I need to go. Thanks for the info." He hung up.

Questions swirled around in Ryan's head. Was that Ethan on the other end of her phone call? Did she leave on her own? Did he hurt her? Or kill her?

Ryan looked up to see Patel staring at him over his shoulder and Porter glancing at him through the rearview. "Well?" the two detectives asked in unison.

Ryan explained what Vanessa had told him about seeing Kate duck into the kitchen.

"Too bad she didn't say anything we don't already know," Patel said.

"Suki, we really need you to think," Porter urged the young woman. "Is there any place you can think of where your brother might have taken Kate? A warehouse? A park? Or a house your brother might go to? Somewhere he used to work maybe?"

"Think!" Ryan demanded.

"I'm trying," Suki snapped back. She paused for a moment. "Our house. Yes, he might have taken her to our house, the one we lived in when our mom died."

"Wouldn't someone else live there now?" Officer Diaz asked.

"No, it's vacant," Suki said. "Yesterday, my brother told me he went by the house, just to look at it for old-time sake. He said he wanted to remember when we were kids and we were happy. He told me it was empty and had a for-sale sign out front. We lost the house after my mom died, but the people who bought it must have lost their jobs or something and lost the house, too."

"So, what's the address?" Patel asked.

"Oh, gosh, that was ten years ago. I was only fourteen."

"You have to remember!" Patel yelled, his eyes wide, staring at her in the back seat. "Think!"

"Well, it was on Queen Anne Hill."

"What was the name of the street?" Patel demanded.

"Let me think. Stop yelling at me and just let me think!" she cried.

Ryan crossed his arms and looked out the window. *Maybe she's already dead.* He shook his head, as if he could shake the thoughts out of it. *No, I have to stay positive. I have to find her.*

190

Then he thought about what Vanessa had said—that Kate put her phone in her bra. *Why?* Normally, she would have stuck it in her pocket or in her purse, but putting it down her bra meant she did it for a reason. It occurred to him that maybe she left her phone on and silenced it so the police could track her by GPS. That would mean she knew she was going to be taken.

"Raj."

"Yeah?" Raj shifted in his seat and looked at Ryan over his shoulder.

"Vanessa said something else. I didn't think anything of it at first, but now—"

"What is it?"

"She said she saw Kate put her phone down her shirt before she went to the kitchen. I think that says she knew she was in danger. Do you think you could get a police tech to track her phone by GPS?"

"Yes, that's a great idea," Raj agreed.

"And what about finding the last person who called her? Could the tech find out who that was and track that phone, too?"

"Probably. Let me give them a call."

"We're almost there," Porter said. "I see flashing lights ahead."

"What now?" Ryan asked.

Patel met his gaze. "Ryan, just sit tight, like you promised."

CHAPTER 17

"Look, there's the ambulance, Raj. The Underground Tour building must be right up ahead." Porter pulled over to the curb. A couple other officers had already blocked off part of the street for the ambulance and police cars.

Porter and Patel jumped out first, grabbing their flashlights. Officer Diaz helped Suki out of the vehicle and kept a firm grasp on her arm while Ryan stood beside the car.

"You stay put," Raj ordered, pointing a finger at Ryan as he and Porter walked off toward the building. If he remained with the car and let the detectives do their job, Patel had said, they would find Whitney sooner and then they could get back to looking for Kate.

The manager had already unlocked the front door for them, turned on the lights, and was waiting for them in the foyer. Diaz escorted her prisoner into the building.

"Suki," the manager said when he saw her, "what have you done?"

She looked at him for a moment, then hung her head and kept walking.

Porter stopped just outside the front door and signaled to the paramedics to follow them with the stretcher, as a gurney would be too difficult to handle going down the stairs and into the underground city. Then he ducked inside.

Raj shot Ryan a warning glance as he held the door for the paramedics, then went inside.

"Miss Henderson," Detective Porter said, "where do we go from here?"

She lifted her head when he called her name. "Down those stairs," she answered, motioning with her right shoulder to the wide set of stairs with peeling green paint which took them to the lower-level souvenir shop.

"Show us where to go," Porter ordered and they disappeared into the lower level."

Left with his thoughts, Ryan did his best not to think the worst. He glanced at his watch. *What's taking them so long?*

He paced beside the car, replaying the evening in his mind. They had kissed at his condo. Would it be their last? Then they went to Whitney's apartment so Kate could change before they went to dinner. They heard voices.

The television! He remembered the TV being on in Suki's room. *Could Ethan have been there?* It made sense. *What if he was still there, hiding, when we were?* A sinking feeling weighed heavily in his chest. *What if Kate had gone alone? He could have killed her right then.*

"That would explain why he called her shortly after that," Ryan said aloud, having an epiphany. "After hearing us talk in his sister's room, he probably became even more agitated, more determined." *Oh, Kate, hold on.*

From his post between the police cruiser and the ambulance, Ryan noticed Officer Diaz come out of the building with Suki in tow. She ushered her to the car and helped her into the back seat. The police woman had just gotten in herself when the paramedics came up carrying a woman on a stretcher. She had short blonde hair and bore a definite resemblance to Kate.

Whitney, she's alive.

"Thank you, thank you, thank you," Whitney cried in a hoarse voice, tears streaking her face. She reached out and grabbed Will's hand. "I thought I was going to die in there."

"You're safe now," Porter assured her, patting her hand. "These paramedics are going to take you to the hospital. They'll check you out and take good care of you. When you're up to it, we'll come by and talk with you. Okay?"

"Okay," she answered in a raspy voice. She nodded and wiped her tears with her hands.

"Can we get this girl some water to drink?" Porter asked the EMTs. "She seems pretty dehydrated."

"Don't worry. We'll take care of her, sir." The paramedics lifted Whitney's body onto the gurney and then maneuvered her into the ambulance.

Ryan rushed up to them. "Is she okay?"

"She seems to be," Raj replied, glancing over at the ambulance. "We'll know more after the docs examine her."

"That's great to hear, Raj. Now we need to find Kate." Ryan hoped his voice conveyed the urgency. He began moving toward the car.

"Where do we start?" Raj asked, as he and Porter started walking back to their vehicle.

Officer Diaz opened the car door and stood up, resting an arm on the door. "I've got something for you," she called out.

Porter and Patel rushed over. "What is it?" Porter asked.

"Suki said she just remembered the name of the street their house was on—Comstock."

"Comstock?" Ryan asked.

"Sound familiar?" Raj questioned as he got into the front passenger seat.

"Definitely. Hang on." Ryan climbed into the backseat and looked up the active homes for sale on the Multiple Listing Service on his cell phone. He found the address for the only home currently for sale on Comstock. It happened to be the home he was interested in buying—the one he'd shown to Kate that first night.

"What are the chances of that?" he muttered.

"The chances of what?" Porter asked, getting in behind the wheel.

~*~

Rousing from unconsciousness, Kate was disoriented and dizzy. She found herself in total darkness, curled up in a cramped space. Feeling movement, bumpy at times, she realized she was in the trunk of a car.

The last thing she remembered was going out to the alley, behind the restaurant, to get instructions from Ethan on how to get Whitney back. At least that's what he told her. Then everything went black.

He must have knocked me out. Her head throbbed and pain was shooting behind her eyes. She struggled to clear the fog in her mind.

The movement of the vehicle stopped. When the engine cut, Kate thought they must be parked. Wherever he was taking her, they must have arrived.

The trunk opened and Ethan pulled her up by her arm. He practically dragged her from the car, through the side gate, to the back of a house. There was something familiar about the place, but she couldn't put her finger on it.

She was not yet steady on her feet, nor was she strong enough to fight back. "Where are we?"

"We're home," he said, grinning. "Do you know how lucky we are? No, of course you don't."

She had no idea what he was talking about. *He must be crazy.*

He pulled her up the stairs. "This is the house I grew up in. You know, the one we lost when you killed our mother. You ruined our lives, Kate McAllister, and you're gonna pay for it."

Kate was terrified. She thought she could try to reason with him. "If you lost the house because of me, how come we're here now? Doesn't it belong to someone else?"

"Shows what you know," he spat. "I came here yesterday to check it out. Lucky me, the house was vacant. Let's just say, I left the door open. After I couldn't do what I'd planned at the apartment today, I knew it would be the perfect place to bring you."

Couldn't do what he'd planned at the apartment today?

Ethan pulled Kate inside the dark house, shoved her to the bare floor in the living room, and loomed over her. Moonlight shone in through the large picture window and the light bounced off the hardwood floor, illuminating the whites of his eyes.

"Why are you doing this?" she asked him. She noticed his dilated pupils and his jittery movements. *He looks like he's high on something.*

"You know exactly why," he shot back.

"I don't." She closed her eyes and moved her head slowly from side to side, still trying to regain full consciousness.

She looked up at him, squinting, as the fog in her mind began to dissipate. *It was him in the apartment today—he left the TV on, not Suki.* Then she remembered he was the one who had phoned her at the restaurant, and she recalled going through the kitchen and out into the back alleyway. It was coming into focus for her. Lying flat on her back, she lifted a hand to the side of her aching head.

"Of course, you do. It's because I have to finish what you started!"

"What I started? I still don't understand," she said.

"It's because you are the high and mighty Kate McAllister, the girl that killed my mother and destroyed my family." An angry sharpness lined his voice.

"What? No!" she responded, shaking her head. "No, Ethan, listen. I didn't *kill* your mother. It was an accident, a terrible accident." Battling to stay calm, she was determined not to let him see her fear.

"It *was* your fault! Stop denying it! After you killed my mom, my dad drank himself out of a job and we lost this house." Ethan paused and looked around the room, as if he was still grieving the loss of the life he once had. "After Dad committed suicide, my sister got shipped off to a stinkin' foster home. And you, Miss Kate McAllister, got off scot-free! Well, you're not going to get away with it anymore. It ends here, tonight."

Her head was pounding with pain as she lay on the hard floor, and his words became a jumble in her mind. None of what he said made sense to her at that point. He sounded like a ranting lunatic, which made her all the more terrified of him.

He pulled a piece of thin rope out of his back pocket. Crouching down, he grabbed one arm and she kicked and scratched at his face with her free hand. He hit her hard with the back of his hand and violently rolled her over onto her stomach.

No longer laying on the aching back of her head, the throbbing began to subside and her thoughts became clearer. Kate mustered all the strength she could to keep her voice even, not wanting to incite this madman further.

"You don't have to do this, Ethan. Please, can't we talk about it?"

The phone in her bra began to vibrate against her breast, which gave her a start. She coughed a few times to cover up the noise and her initial reaction to the vibration. Kate continued to hope that it would help someone locate her.

"We're done talking," he snarled. "There's nothing you could say that can save you now," he said, wrapping the rope around her wrists. "I thought killing your mom and

199

dad would be enough payback," he muttered as he cinched the rope tight, "but it wasn't." He rolled her back over and pulled her into a sitting position on the floor as he stood.

Ethan's admission hit her like a slap in the face. "So, it *was* you that caused their accident." Hot tears rushed to her eyes at the thought of them, victims of his crazy obsession to exact revenge against her.

"I didn't think you knew." He smiled a little, seeming to take some sick pleasure that she knew what he had done.

"I didn't know, not until today." A few drops trickled down her face.

"Hmmm." He frowned and pursed his lips, as if he was disappointed that she hadn't been weighed down under the knowledge of it all this time. "So how'd you find out?"

"I went to the crash site today. There was a blue cap stuck in a bush by the tree they hit, a cap like the one you're wearing now. I put two and two together, just like the police will."

"I don't think so. They're not that smart. Besides, I'll be long gone by the time they find you and your sister."

"My sister? Do you know where my sister is?"

"Maybe," he taunted her.

"Did you take Whitney?"

"Suki took her."

"Suki?"

"Funny, isn't it?" he chuckled.

"Tell me, please. Is my sister alive?"

"Well, I don't know. Probably not." Ethan toyed with Kate, like an animal playing with its prey before he devoured it.

Kate struggled to blink back the bitter tears that were stinging her eyes. On the heels of his blatant admission that he had killed her parents, the thought that he may have also killed her sister was too much to take.

Ethan's glassy eyes lit up. Kate noticed the evidence of his delight at having struck a painful nerve in her, although he appeared to relish the pleasure for only a moment or two before refocusing on why he brought her to this empty place.

"We've wasted enough time talking. Let's finish this thing." Ethan pulled his pearl-handled switchblade out of his back pocket, clicked it open, exposing the long metal blade. "This used to be my father's, and my grandfather's before that." He looked at it lovingly, as if it was the last vestige of the family he once had. "My grandpa brought it back with him from World War II."

"No, Ethan, please!"

The moonlight glinted off the metal as he put his boot on her chest and pushed Kate backwards with force.

She cried in pain, as her back and head slammed down on the hard floor.

He stooped down over her, leaning his knee on her stomach. She gasped for air as his weight pressed on her diaphragm. Terror immobilized her and her throat constricted. She tried to scream. No sound came out of her open mouth.

Wild eyed, he grabbed a handful of her blonde hair in one hand and raised the knife to stab her.

Paralyzed with fear, Kate's eyes were riveted on his. Horrifying scenes flashed in her mind, visions of him stabbing her over and over again, as he released his fury.

~*~

Patel's phone rang. It was the tech guy. The GPS had zeroed in on the house on Comstock. "Well, you were right, Ryan. It is the house you thought it was," he said, hanging up his phone.

They were still at least ten minutes away by car. Porter flipped on the lights and siren. Traffic was dense, bumper to bumper, in this part of town, and with vehicles parked all along the street, there was nowhere for the cars in front to pull over to let the police cruiser through.

Ryan couldn't wait. His adrenaline surged at the confirmation that Kate was so close. He had to get to her! If her phone was still broadcasting a signal, that had to mean that Ethan hadn't found it. He prayed that meant that Kate was still alive.

Patel must have sensed Ryan's desperation because he turned around and made eye contact. "Ryan," he started, "I know what you're thinking, and don't."

Ryan didn't say a word to his friend. The wheels in his head were turning so quickly that he almost didn't hear the warning tone in Patel's voice. Instead, his inner-cop kicked in and he did the only thing he could.

He opened the back door and bolted. *I'm coming, Kate. Just hang on a little longer.*

The last thing he heard as he ran from the car was Porter, "Aw, crap."

~*~

For an instant, the room lit up. Headlights flashed across the picture window. Ethan froze and listened. There was the sound of a car door opening and closing in front of the house.

"Not. A. Word." His voice came in short panting bursts, his knee still pinning her down.

Then Ethan raised his head and stretched to peer out the bottom of the bare front window. With the pressure on her chest momentarily alleviated, Kate lifted her head to see.

There was a dark SUV parked in front and a man getting out. It resembled Ryan's vehicle, and that's when she realized why the house seemed familiar. It was the one Ryan had wanted to show her, but it had been too dark. For a second her heart surged with hope, but it dropped again when she noticed the man go inside the house across the street.

"*Whew*. It's not the cops," he muttered under his breath. His forehead wrinkled with a frown, but he seemed to relax a little, seeing that it was just a neighbor.

Then Ethan's expression changed. The crazed, cold stare came back. "Now, where were we?"

Kate stared at him intently, trying to read his face, searching for a chance to escape. She knew now that that was her only hope. No one had come to help her. It was just her and this madman.

His knife blade flashed with the light from the streetlamp. Kate's fear froze into a lump in her throat. *This is it. I'm going to die,* she thought. *Oh, Whitney, I'm so sorry.*

Just then, there was the sound of rattling at the front door. *The MLS lockbox!* At that instant Kate knew it was Ryan outside.

They both looked toward the front door and they could see Ryan bringing his hands up to cup them around the sides of his face, presumably in an attempt to peek inside the dark house.

Ethan dropped low and frantically dragged Kate to the basement door before Ryan made it inside. "Don't make a sound, or after I kill you, I'll kill your nosey boyfriend."

She nodded.

He pulled her to her feet and down into the basement. He lifted her up and slid her bound wrists over a broken two-by-four in the wall. It was too high for her to get herself free, but if he left her alone long enough...maybe.

"Not a peep," he warned her again. Then Ethan closed his blade and shoved it in his back pocket. "I *could* stab him, but I'm saving my dad's knife just for you, Kate." Hastily, he rummaged around the basement for something else to use to deal with Ryan.

Finding a few loose bricks, he grabbed one and climbed back up the stairs, opening the door just a crack to peer out. He flashed a warning glare at Kate as he slowly eased the door open, not making a sound.

"Ryan!" Kate shouted, but she was too late.

As much as she hoped that Ryan would see Ethan first, the loud *thud* she heard after Ethan stepped through the door told her he had managed to sneak up behind Ryan and had likely smashed the brick against the back of his head, sending him flying to the floor. A sharp crashing noise made her jump, which she imagined was Ethan dropping the brick on the hardwood. When there were no further sounds of a struggle, she assumed that Ryan had been stopped.

Ethan came running down the basement steps, breathing frantically. He unwrapped her wrists from the two-by-four and dragged Kate up the stairs sideways, by her tethered arms. As he headed to the back door, she caught a glimpse of Ryan lying prostrate on the floor. *Is he dead?*

"Ryan!" she called out as Ethan dragged her away, but he remained motionless.

"Come on," Ethan demanded as he pulled her to the car. "Get in." He opened the back door.

She kicked him hard in the shin and turned to bolt.

Cursing at her, he grabbed Kate by her hair and shoved her into the back seat. Then he jumped into the driver's seat, started the engine, and backed down the narrow driveway at a furious pace. Once on the street, he floored it.

CHAPTER 18

KATE BOUNCED AROUND in the backseat, worrying about Ryan and trying to think of a way out. She worked at the ropes binding her wrists, but they weren't budging.

Ethan eyed her in the rearview mirror. "Don't worry, Kate," he said. "When things didn't work out at the apartment earlier, I figured I'd better have another backup plan if things didn't work out at the house. Killing you at Kerry Park is just as good, I figure. You know Kerry Park, don't you? Just down here a few blocks from the house. It was one of my parents' favorite places to go."

She didn't say anything, just studied him, looking for a solution.

In the mirror, she could see Ethan get a wistful look in his eyes. "My mom and dad loved Kerry Park, how it was terraced into the side of Queen Anne Hill, you know, with that long set of concrete steps from the street below up to the top tier. That was their favorite part—the top tier. You could really get a good look at the Space Needle and downtown Seattle from there. I remember Suki and I used to play on the lower tiers, on the swings and the playground equipment."

Kate watched, as Ethan's face twisted again into the crazed one she was now familiar with. "That was before you ruined everything!" he yelled over his shoulder. "If I can't kill you at our old house, this is the second best place."

Trembling, Kate pondered the irony. Not only that she had come here with Ryan, but that it had been *her* parents' favorite spot, as well.

~*~

Ryan lay on the wood floor, coming to as he heard his phone ringing in his pocket. Weak from the blow to the head, he struggled to sit up. Leaning back on one hand, he answered his phone.

"This is Ryan," he said, feeling a few drops of blood trickling down his neck.

"Ryan, this is Raj. What were you thinking, man?"

"I was thinking I needed to rescue Kate."

"Well, as much as I'd like to chew you out right now for running off, I'm not going to—I'll do that later. We have the GPS location of Kate's phone. It's not at the house on Comstock like it was—it appears to be nearby. Where are you?"

"I'm at the house on Comstock. I think Ethan was here."

"What makes you say that?"

"Because the house was dark when I got here, but there was a car in the driveway. So, I used my lockbox key and let myself in to look around."

"You shouldn't have done that."

"I know, I know. I wish I hadn't," Ryan said. "I got hit from behind and knocked out."

"Are you okay?"

"Yeah, a little dizzy, but I'll be all right."

"Good. You were lucky."

"I know."

"Was Kate at the house?"

"She could have been."

"Hang on." Raj put Ryan on hold, then he came back. "Well, it looks like the GPS is showing Kate's phone at Kerry Park on West Highland Drive."

"Let's hope she's with it."

"That's all we've got to go on, so we're headed over there right now. We're just a few minutes away."

"I'll meet you over there."

"No, Ryan. You sit tight, and I'll send someone to pick you up."

"But, Raj, I—"

"You heard me. Sit tight. I mean it."

~*~

Ethan stopped at the curb along the narrow strip of park. Since it was late and there was an icy chill in the air, the tiny park was empty. He yanked Kate out of the car and pulled her across the park to the overlook railing near the top of the concrete stairway. Peering over the railing to the playground area below, Kate's heart began to pound hard against her chest and her knees felt shaky, as if they might give out.

"Ethan, don't do this. Please." She glanced beyond the railing again.

"Listen to you beg. You make me sick."

"Come on, you don't have to do this."

"You didn't give my mother a chance to beg for mercy when you slammed your big fat SUV into her little car."

"It was an accident. I keep trying to tell you—it was an accident!" she screamed, her lips trembling.

"Accident or not, it was your fault!" he yelled back, tightening his grasp on her arm. "You ruined my whole life."

"Ethan, please," she implored. Physically and emotionally exhausted, she was losing the battle to control her tears. "That's why the police never charged me, it wasn't my fault," she said, trying to explain between sobs. "Please...believe me. I, I beg you, don't do this."

"Shut up! If it hadn't been for you, I'd still have my family!" His behavior was becoming more erratic and agitated. His eyes darted around as he wiped his nose on his sleeve.

I can't just crumble and let him kill me. Maybe if I can keep him talking...you can do this, Kate.

She took a deep breath, willing her sobs to stop. She was determined to rally her courage and get more power over the situation. "What do you mean you'd still have your family?"

Ethan did not answer her. He had that faraway look in his eyes again. Was he thinking back to a fond childhood memory?

Then, as fast as the faraway look settled on his face it was gone, replaced by a vicious snarl. "You know exactly what I mean!"

Kate remembered him saying something about his father back at the house, but it didn't make any sense to her at the time, something about his father killing himself. She wasn't aware of anything having to do with his family, except for his mother dying in the car crash.

"Because of you, my father began drinking and killed himself. Suki got sent to live with a freakin' foster family!" he barked.

But she didn't know about their father's drinking problem or his suicide. How could she have known what had become of Mr. Henderson or that Suki had been sent to a foster home? After the investigation, she had no further contact with the Henderson family. In her wildest dreams, she could never have imagined that the family's last remaining members would become obsessed with taking revenge on her.

Even though the accident was not her fault, as a teenager Kate had gone through a year of therapy to help her cope with the guilt over taking a life. With the investigation of the accident behind her, and with the help of her therapist, she had worked hard to move on with her life.

"I honestly didn't know anything about that."

"Are you serious?" he asked, with biting sarcasm.

"I am serious." *Keep him talking.* "Tell me what happened."

"Are you trying to say you didn't know my dad started drinking after the accident and lost his job and killed himself?"

"No, I didn't know. How could I? Think about it. I didn't have any contact with your family once I was cleared of the accident."

"It was after you killed my mom that all the crap happened with my dad. Because of that, I had to quit school."

"I didn't know," Kate kept saying.

"I would've finished college and had a good job and a nice family. Now look at me, look what I've turned into!"

And that's my fault?

"And my sister, oh, my sister," he shook his head and chuckled in disgust. "She wouldn't have had to be raised by those freakin' foster parents. That Mr. DiMarco was a real peach. We could have had a good life, Suki and me, but you took that all away from us!" he screamed, his eyes widening. "And nobody made you pay for it. Nobody!"

Take a breath. Keep him talking.

"Listen, Ethan. You already paid me back, remember?" She tried to reason with him, acutely aware of the nearness of the long line of cement steps leading down to the street below.

He shook his head violently.

"Yes, you told me you killed my folks." Her throat tightened. "And probably my sister." Her voice cracked as she spoke. "Isn't that enough? Please say that's enough."

"No! It's not enough," he growled. "I thought it would be, but it's not." He shook his head again. "My life was ruined, and you're sitting pretty in Los Angeles with your cushy job and your expensive stuff."

"Please don't do this. Would your mom want you to do this?"

"Shut up! Don't talk about my mom!" He slapped her across the face. "You're just trying to stall. Well, it's not gonna work, princess. I'm done talking!"

He attempted to push her nearer to the steps with his body, but she planted her feet and pushed back. She leaned into him with her full weight and resisted with every bit of strength she possessed.

"Don't do this, Ethan!" she pleaded, gritting her teeth.

"I have to. An eye for an eye, ya' know?"

At the sound of car doors closing, Ethan spun around to see. Because Kate was leaning into him, she fell off balance as he swung her around with him, and she hit the ground. He pulled her to her feet as the detectives approached.

In the background, Kate noticed a female officer helping his handcuffed sister out of the back seat of their car. In a flash, he whipped out the knife, clicked it open, and held it dangerously close to her neck.

In response, both detectives instantly drew their guns.

"Ethan! Stop!" Suki hollered as she and the police rushed toward him. Officer Diaz pulled hard on Suki's arm to stop her when she was within fifteen feet from her brother. Suki tried to shake free from her grip, but Diaz held firm.

"What are you doin' here, Suki?" Ethan questioned, visibly irritated things were not going as he had planned.

"Trying to stop you before you do something we'll both regret."

"It's too late."

"No! We were wrong, Ethan. We were wrong. You have to let Kate go."

"What are you talking about?" his voice rising with agitation.

"I found out today that the crash wasn't Kate's fault after all."

"I don't believe you. The police are messin' with you, Sis. They've twisted your mind, brainwashed you, but I'm not falling for it."

"Ethan, listen to me. We blamed Kate for so many years, planning our revenge. It was our thing, what kept us close. I know it's hard to admit now, but we got it wrong."

"Why are you saying this now?" Ethan shouted, wild-eyed and jittery, moving from foot to foot.

"Do you remember Mrs. DiMarco? My foster mother?"

"Yeah. So what? What's she got to do with anything?"

"She saw the police bringing me in, on the TV, and came to the police station. She brought a copy of Dad's suicide note that she'd been holding all these years. He explained in the note how everything was *his* fault."

"I don't believe you," Ethan said, tightening his hold on Kate. "I don't remember any suicide note."

"There was. Mrs. DiMarco's been holding on to it."

"How do you know it's real? Huh? How? It's probably just a trick."

"That's what I thought too, at first, so I looked at it for a long time. I know it was Dad's handwriting."

"What did he say?" Ethan asked skeptically.

"He said he was sorry for ruining everything. The day Mom died she found out he was having an affair."

"I don't believe it! Dad would never do that to Mom!" Ethan erupted, all the while holding on to Kate's arm and

214

brandishing the knife. The long cement staircase was just a few feet behind them, and Ethan could easily throw her down the steps at any moment.

"She was drinking when he came home and they had a big fight. Mom got in her car and left. *She's* the one who ran the stop sign."

"No, no. That can't be right."

"Dad said he was sorry for losing his job and the house. He said it was all *his* fault." Suki said. "I know you don't want to believe it. I didn't want to believe it either, but it's true. Please, Ethan, put the knife down and let Kate go."

"No, Sis, I can't believe it. I won't! Not in a million years. How can you even say that?"

"I wouldn't lie to you, Ethan."

"The cops probably put you up to it, didn't they? What the hell did they promise you to get you to turn on me?"

"Nothing. They didn't promise me anything. I'm here because I don't want them to kill you."

"Kill me?" he snickered.

"Yes! If you hurt Kate, they'll shoot you down. You know they will." Suki paused for a moment, releasing a long sigh. "We were wrong, Ethan. We were just plain wrong. Now, please, please...let Kate go." She took a couple of steps closer to her brother, dragging Officer Diaz up with her.

"No, you're wrong!"

"Come one, Ethan, people make mistakes. Dad made a mistake, a bad one. Then, everything else just started falling apart around him—around us."

"I'm not listening to this." He shook his head back and forth. "I know it was Kate's fault. It was *all* her fault."

"No, Ethan, no," Suki argued, "it wasn't. I'm telling you...she's innocent in all of this."

Ethan jerked Kate closer in front of him, into a chokehold, and held the knife against her neck.

Feeling the sting of the sharp blade against her skin, her body stiffened and her eyes grew big as saucers, terrified that he was about to slit her throat before the police could do anything to save her.

"Put the guns down or I'll kill her right now," Ethan demanded. "I mean it!" He was jumpy and highly agitated. "If I die, she dies too."

Porter and Patel held their ground, neither lowering their weapons. The four back-up officers, who had quietly fanned out behind the detectives, also kept their guns laser focused on Ethan.

"My life is over, Sis, either way," Ethan told her. His voice was starting to sound frighteningly resigned.

From Kate's vantage point, his eyes seemed riveted on the drawn guns. She felt him edging her closer to the steep concrete steps. She fought to keep her feet planted.

"So, why not end it all right here, right now?" he asked. "Kate McAllister started this whole thing, ruined my family and my life. I've got nothing left."

Kate noticed movement in her peripheral vision. Was someone climbing the concrete steps in an attempt to save her? Could it be Ryan? Her heart pounded in her ears and she could hardly breathe. Would Ethan kill them both?

"No!" Suki screamed.

Thwack!

Kate heard the chilling sound and felt the weight of Ethan collapsing, dragging her down to the ground with him.

Ryan had crept silently up the stairs, and then wait for the opportune moment to crack Ethan on the back of his head with the brick he found on the floor at the house. It was only fitting payback, seeing how Ethan had a penchant for doing the same to others.

Porter and Patel rushed over to Ethan while he was down. Porter kicked the knife out of Ethan's hand and pulled him off of Kate. Patel bent down and put two fingers against Ethan's neck, checking for a pulse, and made sure he was breathing.

Ethan began to come around. Porter immediately jumped on him, put a knee in his back, and secured his hands with cuffs. Diaz kept a tight hold of Suki's arm, even though she tried to pull free and run to her brother.

"Don't hurt him!" Suki hollered.

"Okay, dirt bag, get on your feet." Porter yanked Ethan to a standing position and supported him as he escorted his woozy prisoner to one of the police cars.

Kate struggled to get on her feet and Ryan rushed to her aid. He reached down and helped her up. Raj offered to cut her ropes off with his pocketknife.

Once free, Kate flung her arms around Ryan's body and he wrapped his arms around her. Within seconds, his lips were on hers and they were locked in a passionate embrace.

Raj cleared his throat.

Realizing they were not alone, Kate and Ryan untangled their lips and each took a breath, but neither wanted to let go of the other.

"I thought you were dead," she told him, tears streaming down her cheeks. She laid her head against his chest. "I saw you lying there on the floor, you weren't moving, and my heart just about leapt out of my chest."

"I wasn't sure I'd ever see you alive again, either," he responded in his warm, deep voice.

She looked up at him and he studied her face.

"One minute we're about to have a nice dinner and the next thing I know you've disappeared into thin air."

"Okay then...I'm guessing you guys would like some privacy," Raj said, shoving his hands in his pockets as he backed away and wandered over to his car.

"Thanks, Raj," Ryan muttered, his eyes not leaving Kate's. "I never want to lose you again." He leaned his forehead against hers.

Then suddenly she pulled back from him, her eyes growing wide. "My sister! Ryan, what about Whitney?"

Worry washed over her. In that instant, she realized she had been out of touch with the world for hours. The last she'd learned, before her abduction, was that the detectives were questioning Suki at the police station. No one had told her anything about Whitney yet.

"Whitney, yes. Sorry, I've just been focused on rescuing you from that psycho."

"And I'm incredibly grateful for that, but I have to know—is there any news about my sister?"

"I know she's alive."

"Thank God. Where was she?"

"In the Underground Tour somewhere. Suki led the police to her, and the paramedics took her to the hospital."

Kate's hand flew to her throat. "Oh, Ryan, how did she look?"

"She looked rough, but at least she's alive. Maybe Raj can tell you more." Ryan turned and called out to Patel as he was beginning to get into the car. "Hey, Raj! Wait up!"

Ryan wrapped his arm around Kate's waist and walked her over to the Crown Victoria. Suki sat sullen in the back seat with Officer Diaz, and Porter was starting the engine. Patel paused for a moment and climbed back out.

"What's up?" he asked, closing the door.

"No one's filled Kate in on what's happening with her sister. Can you tell us what's going on?"

Raj took a few minutes and explained to her how they rescued her sister and which hospital she was taken to.

"So Whitney's all right?" Kate asked.

"She looked okay to me when the paramedics were putting her in the ambulance, maybe a bit weak and shaky. She'd been drugged to keep her sedated. There was a little blood on her face when we found her, but she didn't seem to have any obvious injuries. The doctors are checking her out now."

"Oh, thank you!" Kate squealed and gave the detective a quick hug. "I have to go see her."

"After we drop Suki off at the station, Porter and I are headed over to the hospital to check on her and see if she's up to talking."

"We'll need to catch a ride over there, too," Ryan said, as he glanced over at Kate.

Raj shouted and waved to one of the uniformed officers. "Hey, can you give these two a ride to the hospital?"

He gave Kate and Ryan a thumbs-up.

"Johnson will give you guys a lift. And hey, Ryan, get your head looked at while you're there." He grinned and then turned to leave.

Kate suddenly remembered something. "Detective, wait! I have something to tell you. You, too, Ryan."

"What?" Patel asked.

"When Ethan held me at the house, he admitted that he had caused my parents' auto accident."

"That's what you thought, when we were at the crash site on Bainbridge Island," Ryan said.

"He admitted that? Why would he just come out and tell you that?" Patel questioned.

"Because he was going to kill me. At that point, he didn't care, I guess. Besides, I think he thought I knew all this time."

"That means he's not just a kidnapper, he's also a murderer," Raj said. "Hopefully, his confession and that cap are enough to get a murder charge. We'll need more to get a conviction, but it's a start." Raj reached out and put his hand on Kate's shoulder for a moment. "Thanks for letting me know. I'm sorry you had to be the one to discover that."

"I just hope he's going to pay for what he did to my folks."

"Yes, he's going to learn that revenge has a price," Raj told them.

"It shows what a cold-hearted killer he is," Ryan added, as he took Kate's hand. "He would have killed you."

"If it wasn't for you coming to the house…" Kate closed her eyes, remembering how the hatred had contorted Ethan's face into a mask of pure evil. She shook away the memory and squeezed Ryan's hand. "He grabbed me by my hair and was about to stick a knife in my chest when you came to the door. Instead, he dragged me down to the basement."

"Oh, Kate, I didn't realize…"

"After he knocked you out, he decided to kill me at this park instead."

"And you sneaking up the steps behind him saved her again," Raj added. "You're a hero, my friend," Raj said, with a little grin.

"You certainly are *my* hero," Kate chimed in, flashing a grateful smile at her rescuer.

"Okay, okay," Ryan said, raising his hands in surrender. "That's enough."

"I better get going. Porter's got the car running, and he doesn't like waiting on me." Raj opened the car door and started to get in. "I'll let him know about the murder charge."

"Murder charge?" Porter asked in the background.

"See you guys at the hospital."

CHAPTER 19

RYAN PUT HIS ARM AROUND KATE and they watched as the detectives drove off. Another patrol car waited for them down the street.

She turned toward him and he wrapped her in his arms. Standing in his cosseted embrace, Kate breathed him in—his scent, his words, his strength. He pushed a strand of her hair back from her face and tenderly kissed her cheek.

Kate had only known this man for three days, yet her feelings for him had grown in quantum leaps during that short but intense time. She was sure now that he felt the same.

She took his arm as they walked toward the waiting police cruiser. She thought back over the last few days, which were a whirlwind of drama and emotions. It was amazing to her how much life a person can pack into such a short span of time. Almost from the moment she met Ryan, he had become a strong force in her life, giving her support and help at every turn—from her sister's disappearance, to identifying the dead body in Boise, to facing her parents' crash site, to being kidnapped and almost killed.

After all of that, she was dramatically rescued—by him, no less. If he hadn't come to the house looking for her, if he had followed Detective Patel's directive to sit tight, Kate knew she would be dead.

Reaching the car, he held the door open for her in his chivalrous way. She paused before getting into the vehicle.

"We'll be just a few minutes," she said to the officer behind the wheel.

"Take your time," he said.

She shut the door and turned to face Ryan.

"I thought you were in a hurry to see your sister," he said, apparently puzzled by her pause.

"I am, but I want to say something first." Kate leaned back a little and rested her hip against the side of the vehicle. "Things are going to get hectic at the hospital. Everyone's focus will be on Whitney, as it should be. I'm sure there's a flurry of doctors and nurses checking her out right now, so we have a few minutes."

"All right."

"Ryan," she began, gazing up into his gentle green eyes, "I hardly know how to thank you."

"You don't need to thank me. I was happy to help—I needed to," he answered, stepping in closer, as if he was going to kiss her.

As he leaned in, she put a hand on his chest, not to stop him, but to feel his strength. Looking up at him, she grabbed hold of his shirt where she had rested her hand, pulling him down to her, and kissed him long and slow. She never wanted to let him go.

His arms wrapped around her, and she could feel the beat of his heart as her body pressed against his. She had never felt like this about any other man, and her head was spinning.

When their lips parted, they both struggled to catch their breath. Ryan was the first to speak and the deep feelings of his heart spilled out. "I can't stand the thought of you going back to Los Angeles, Kate. I don't want to lose you."

Studying his adoring face for a moment, she reached up, tenderly putting a hand on his cheek. "Don't worry, you're not going to lose me."

"What do you mean?" he asked, a look of hope spreading across his face.

"I mean I'm moving back to Seattle. I want to be close to my sister, and to you—if you want me." The corners of her mouth turned up into an optimistic smile.

"If I want you? Are you kidding me? I'm falling in love with you." His lips were on hers once more, this time with more urgency and hunger than ever before.

Coming up for air, Kate pulled in a deep breath and responded. "I'd be a fool to go back to Los Angeles and leave behind what we've started here."

As he leaned in for another kiss, she put her fingers gently to his lips. "But, we should probably go somewhere more private to continue this conversation."

"Conversation?"

"Get a room!" a scruffy teenager called out from the sidewalk as he flew by on his skateboard.

"My thoughts exactly," Ryan agreed, eyeing Kate with an impish grin.

"Ryan!" Kate chastened, blushing at the thought.

"Okay, we'll go to the hospital first. Then we'll talk about the room."

THE END

Thank you so much for reading my book,

Three Days in Seattle.

I hope you thoroughly enjoyed it.

Debra Burroughs

The highest compliment an author can receive is in the form of a great review, especially if that review is posted on Amazon.com.

~*~

If you'd like to read an excerpt from

**The Scent of Lies,
a Paradise Valley Mystery Book 1**

Just turn the page…

The Scent of Lies

"Oh, what a tangled web we weave when first we practice to deceive."

~ Sir Walter Scott

PROLOGUE

Life has a way of not turning out the way you had planned, of taking you down roads you had no intention of ever going. Moving in unexpected twists and turns, some bends in the road make you stronger, while others can destroy you.

***

"OH, GOD!" THE HOUSEKEEPER GASPED and split the air with a horrifying scream as she discovered the lady of the house kneeling beside her husband who lay on the floor, bleeding.

The wife's gaze flew toward the housekeeper's shriek, her eyes wide and wet, and in her hand was a large bloody knife. She was clothed in a creamy satin robe, the front smeared red with blood. Her attention drifted back to her husband and her flowing dark hair hung heavy around her shoulders as she leaned over the man, sobbing.

"Help me," he whispered almost imperceptibly, terror shimmering in his dark eyes, trying to grab hold of his wife's wrist.

"Ricardo," the woman moaned, shaking her head, as if she was trying to wake from this nightmare. "This can't be happening."

"Delia…" he sputtered breathlessly.

"Marcela, call nine-one-one!" she ordered.

"Ay, Dios mio," the housekeeper cried, standing frozen in the doorway.

"For heaven's sake, Marcela, go call the police!" the wife screeched, "before my husband is dead."

The Scent of Lies

CHAPTER ONE
Friends, Husbands, and Lovers

"BABE, IT'S TIME TO GET UP," Emily Parker muttered sweetly, sleepily stretching her arm out to her husband's side of the bed, searching for his warmth. At the sensation of the crisply cold sheets, her hand recoiled. Flipping back the covers, she sat up and shook her head. After all this time, she still caught herself reaching out for him.

It was late on a lazy Saturday morning. Sleeping in was so unlike her, but after tossing restlessly in the night, with disturbing dreams of her late husband floating in and out of her mind, she hadn't drifted off to sleep until the wee hours of the morning.

Now, after a quick shower, she stood in the middle of her overflowing walk-in closet, looking for something to wear for a celebratory lunch with her best friends. She surveyed the racks of clothes, unable to make up her mind. "This isn't brain surgery, Emily. Pick something," she

3

muttered as she rifled through the clothes on the hangers, but nothing.

With thoughts of her late husband fresh in her mind, she glanced at his side of the closet. "Oh, Evan," she sighed. Everything was exactly as he had left it that final morning six months ago. Still, she had not been able to bring herself to get rid of his things.

Sometimes she simply needed to feel him near, so she would drape herself in one of his shirts or sweaters and breathe in his scent. Today would be one of those times. Compelled as she was by her dreams, her desire to feel close to him won out over her need to hurry and get dressed.

She buried her face in a navy blue hooded sweatshirt hanging on the rack. Breathing in the lingering trace of his rugged masculinity brought him vividly to her mind. She couldn't help herself, she still missed him so much—his crooked smile, the warmth of his strong arms wrapped around her, and the glorious way he made her feel when they made love.

Emily tugged the sweatshirt off the hanger and shrugged it on, hoping for some emotional comfort. Feeling surrounded by his presence, she zipped it up and stuck her hands in the pockets, surprised to feel the crackling of paper in one of them. She pulled out a small folded note. Her curiosity piqued and she opened it. In blue ink, the name Delia and a phone number was scrawled in the cursive penmanship of a woman.

Delia? She frowned at the note. *Who is Delia?* Was she a client, an informant, a friend—a lover? As fast as the thought about her possibly being Evan's lover popped into her head, she pushed it right out again. She'd always had

The Scent of Lies

complete trust in her husband. They had been absolutely happy, that is until the horrible night he was killed. He'd never given her any reason to suspect he had ever been unfaithful to her.

I'm just being silly.

Her cell phone beeped a reminder, telling her she had spent far too long wallowing in Evan's clothes. Now she really needed to hurry and get dressed for her lunch date. She and her girlfriends were celebrating five years from the day they all first met and began what had grown into a close circle of friends. She loved those women, but if she was late, they'd never let her hear the end of it.

She grabbed a pair of white slacks that she knew would show off her slim figure and added a silk turquoise blouse that everyone said set off her dazzling greenish-blue eyes and her head of tousled honey-blonde curls. Emily stepped into her trendy Espadrilles, grabbed her oversized leather purse, and flew out the door.

Her friends had chosen the Blue Moon Café—the current hotspot in Paradise Valley—known for its gourmet menu and outdoor patio that offered a breathtaking view of the river. Emily swung her white Volvo sedan into a parking space in the crowded lot. As she approached the front door, she spotted her party already seated at a table under a large blue umbrella on the breezy patio.

She made her way through the bustling restaurant, lively with laughter and conversation, people talking about what was going on in their lives. Delicious smells wafted through the air as servers carried trays laden with plates of food and upbeat music filled the place.

As Emily stepped out onto the sunny patio, the girls were chatting away. "Hello, ladies." She eased the empty chair out and tucked herself into the group.

Camille patted Emily's hand. "You're late. Is something wrong?"

Like a mother hen to the girls, Camille Hawthorne was a bit older than the others, having a daughter in high school and a son in college. Her looks would not give her age away, though, and she wore her fiery red hair in a cropped and spiky style. But her husband, Jonathan, a sales executive for a local corporation, was the only one who could get away with calling her *Red*.

"I know, I know. I'm sorry. I got a little distracted and lost track of the time." Emily scooted her chair closer to the table, flashing her friend a playful grin.

"We were just concerned, Emily. You're never late." Isabel Martinez tossed her long dark curls over her shoulder. As an FBI financial analyst, Isabel was matter-of-fact and to the point. Usually dressed in a business suit, she appeared relaxed in her jeans and knit top.

"Well, y'all know I'm the one who's always late," Maggie Sullivan admitted in her fading Texas accent, twirling a strand of long blonde hair around her finger. Truthfully, Maggie had a bad habit of being late for almost everything, except for appointments with her clients. As a fitness trainer, she was obsessive when it came to two things—her looks and her business. Tall and leggy with generous breasts and a tiny waistline, Emily always thought Maggie resembled a Barbie doll.

"You said it, not me," Isabel replied to Maggie, while looking over the menu.

6

The Scent of Lies

Camille leaned over toward Emily and asked, "Is everything all right?"

"Yes, I'm fine." Emily placed her napkin in her lap and lowered her voice. "I was standing in my closet trying to decide what to wear and—"

"Yes, I've been known to stand there for half an hour trying to figure out what to put on," Camille interrupted.

"No, that wasn't it." Emily's gaze lowered briefly, considering how much she should tell her. "You see, I couldn't make up my mind so my eyes wandered over to Evan's side of the closet. It was like his clothes were calling to me and I had this overwhelming urge to be close to him."

"Oh, I see," Camille raised her brows, "an overwhelming urge." She took hold of Emily's hand, giving it a light squeeze. "That's totally understandable, Em. You still miss him."

"It probably sounds silly, but I just wanted to smell his scent again, feel a part of him. I grabbed one of his sweatshirts and breathed it in and it brought back such a rush of memories."

"Oh, Emily," Camille sighed.

"So I put the sweatshirt on. That lingering scent—it was like he's still here with me. I miss him so much, Cam." Emily felt herself being pulled back into the moment, her hand fluttered to her chest and her eyes tingled as tears filled them. She sent her gaze flying out over the river, not wanting her friends to see. Fortunately, Maggie and Isabel were engaged in their own conversation.

"Are you okay?" Camille asked, putting a hand on Emily's shoulder.

Emily nodded and drew a deep breath, willing the tears back. Her gaze returned to Camille. "I suddenly remembered how I felt when he held me, when he kissed me...when he made love to me."

"Oh my, Emily," Camille giggled nervously, fanning herself with her napkin, as her face reddened.

The giggle drew Maggie's and Isabel's attention and a blush of embarrassment heated Emily's cheeks. "And that's how the time just slipped away," she muttered to Camille, looking down at her menu, wanting to move on to another topic.

"You'll never get over him if you don't start letting go, Emily. It's been six months," Camille said, appearing not to have caught the hint that Emily wanted to stop talking about it. "Don't you think you should start packing up his things so you can at least begin to move on with your life?"

Maybe Camille was right, but Emily wasn't ready.

"Evan was a wonderful man, Em—really he was."

Wonderful man? Emily had never doubted it before, but what about the note from some mysterious woman named Delia that she had found in Evan's pocket. She hoped he really was as wonderful as everyone thought.

Camille continued. "But he's been gone for a while now and you're still here. You deserve to be happy." She looked around the table for support. "Don't you agree, girls?"

"Yes, Emily," Maggie chimed in, "it is time you start havin' some fun again, girl."

The Scent of Lies

Isabel rushed to Emily's defense. "Don't push her, maybe she's not ready. Six months isn't that long, really."

Emily looked over at Isabel and offered her a smile of appreciation. That was enough talk about Evan. After the night she'd had dreaming about him and his murder, and then finding the suspicious note, it was time for a new subject and she wasn't waiting for anyone else to change it. "So, what should we order?" She picked up her menu and began looking over the offerings.

"Nothin' too fattenin'," Maggie warned.

Emily's gaze flew around the busy patio. "Where's our waitress?"

A young woman appeared at their table, pad and pen in hand. She greeted them and introduced herself while they scanned the menus. "What can I get for you ladies?"

"Excuse me," Emily said, raising her gaze to the girl, "did you say your name was Delia?"

"No," the server replied, "my name is Amelia."

Emily gave her mind a mental shake. She had to find out who this Delia woman was so she could put the suspicions to rest. "Amelia, I'll have the sea bass."

"That sounds good," Camille closed her menu and looked up at the young woman. "How is that prepared?"

"Um, sautéed, I think," she replied sheepishly. "Sorry, I'm new here."

"Don't pay any attention to her," Isabel said to the waitress, frowning at her fiery-haired friend. "She's a chef, so she can be very particular. I'm sure however it's cooked will be fine."

"I guess you're right, Isabel," Camille conceded, handing her menu to the girl. "I will have the sea bass too."

"Just a garden salad for me, please, Balsamic vinaigrette on the side," Maggie ordered. "I have to watch my girlish figure, y' know." She patted her flat tummy.

At thirty-six, Maggie never tried to hide the fact that she was proud that she still possessed the slender figure she'd had when she was a twenty-two-year-old starlet in Hollywood. As a young single mother, she had moved there from Texas with her little boy, trying to get into the movies. Unfortunately, her big break never materialized. So, leaving her deadbeat husband behind, she and her son moved north to Idaho, where her brother and his family lived. She'd worked hard, learned all she could about fitness and training, eventually opening her own business as a personal trainer.

"Hmm," Isabel tapped her finger against her lips. "I'll have the Kobe beef burger, and I'd like the seasoned oven fries with that."

"Isabel, that's a ton of fat and calories," Maggie pointed out.

"I know, I know—but it tastes so good. Besides, I ordered it just to bug you, my friend," Isabel teased.

"You would." Maggie grimaced.

Isabel carried a few extra pounds and often promised her friend she'd work to take them off when she had time, but with her demanding job at the FBI, she never seemed to find the time.

"You are what you eat, Isabel," Maggie told her for the thousandth time.

"Well, maybe I should eat a skinny person, then." Isabel flashed a mischievous smile. "But I don't see that on the menu."

"There's just no point talkin' to you about it." Maggie rolled her eyes and shook her head.

"Exactly."

The waitress collected the rest of the menus. "Thank you, ladies. I'll be back shortly with your food."

Emily took a sip of her ice water, wanting to let someone else be the topic of discussion. "So, what's new in your world, Camille?"

"Oh, girls," Camille's face lit up and her hands flitted about, "I have the most exciting news! You know that big candle business that's expanding and building all those new warehouses and office buildings down by the railroad tracks?"

"You mean Heaven Scent?" Isabel offered.

"Yes, that's the one." Camille wagged a perfectly manicured finger at her friend. "They're also expanding into a new line of bath products and they're having a huge launch party. Guess who they've hired to plan and cater the event?" Camille sat back with a smug grin.

"Hmm, let me think." Isabel tapped her chin mockingly. "Who could it be?"

"Me, you silly." Camille patted Isabel's arm. "Oh, I'm so thrilled I was chosen!"

"Wow, that's a big job," Maggie said. "Kudos, my friend."

"Yes, that's fantastic," Emily chimed in. "Congratulations!"

"Thank you all." Camille smiled broadly. "It's going to be fabulous," she said, waving her hand across the air with a flourish. "But enough about me, what's going on with the rest of you?" She glanced from face to face. "Maggie?"

"I'm happy to report my fitness trainin' business is goin' well. Oh, and I just have to tell y'all that I have the most gorgeous, delicious new client. He's tall, dark and oh-so-handsome," Maggie gushed.

"Sounds like you'd like him to be more than a client, Maggie." Isabel raised a questioning brow.

"Maybe." She giggled.

"He's not married, is he?" Isabel asked suspiciously.

"I don't think so. He doesn't wear a wedding ring and he hasn't mentioned a wife."

"You ought to make sure, Maggie, before you start getting all dreamy over him," Camille warned.

"Yes, Mama," Maggie deferred sarcastically.

"Well, I'm working on a big case," Isabel said. "You might remember from the news when George Semanski was arrested for killing that family in eastern Oregon. We're building a case against him, and he'll be going to trial in a few months."

"Oh my gosh, Isabel," Maggie exclaimed, her blue eyes wide. "What an awful thing for someone to do."

"Why is the FBI involved?" Emily questioned.

"Because after killing the family, Semanski kidnapped the neighbor's kid—or I should say he *allegedly* kidnapped the neighbor's kid—and took him across state lines, which makes it an FBI matter," Isabel explained.

"The story just gets worse," Maggie uttered.

Camille patted Maggie's hand in a comforting way before turning her attention to Emily. "What about you?"

The Scent of Lies

"Me?" Emily would have said things were fine until this morning, but the niggling suspicions about Delia wouldn't leave her alone. Could Evan have possibly been unfaithful to her?

"Yes, you. How's your job going?" Isabel asked.

"Well, I guess my real estate business is doing *okay*." Thankfully they were only asking about her work.

"Not great?" Camille asked, sticking out her bottom lip sympathetically.

"More like limping along," Emily answered truthfully, relieved to put her mind on something else. "I have a young couple I'll be showing homes to later this afternoon. I'm *really* hoping they buy today, because Lord knows I could certainly use the commission right now. A couple of my deals are set to close in the next few weeks—fingers crossed—but there are not nearly as many as there used to be."

"Are you still paying the lease on Evan's old office?" Isabel asked.

Emily grimaced. "Yes, I'm on the hook for another year, unfortunately."

"Ouch," Isabel responded.

"And because it's such an old building, subleasing is next to impossible," Emily went on. "The place is practically vacant as it is."

The server returned with a plate in each hand and another server followed with the rest of the food, setting the plates down in front of each of the women.

Isabel took a whiff of her burger and fries. "Mmm, it smells delicious."

"Yes, it does, and everything looks great too,"
Camille said with a nod. "Thank you, miss."

"I'll be back to check on you ladies a little later.
Enjoy." Amelia moved on to another table.

As soon as she left, Emily gently clinked her knife
against her water glass a few times to draw her friends'
attention.

"In honor of celebrating the five-year anniversary of
the day we met, I would like to make a toast." Emily
raised her glass. The other women picked up their glasses,
as well. "I want to thank each of you for being there for
me when I needed you most this last year, after Evan died,
and for us all being there for each other through all the
many ups and downs of our lives. You are the best friends
any woman could have, and I love you all!"

"Here's to all of us!" Camille exclaimed and they
each took a sip of their drinks. "Thank you, Emily. That
was so sweet." She set her glass down. "Now girls, why
don't we take a walk down memory lane?"

"Memory lane? What do you mean?" Emily asked, as
she picked up her fork to dig into her fish.

"It's been a long time since that special day. I thought
it would be fun to talk about it a little. Do you girls
remember much about the day we first met?" Camille
glanced around the table. "And why you were there?"

"Of course," Isabel answered, munching on one of
her oven fries. "You were holding a cooking class at your
catering shop and we came to learn how to cook."

"You were all such newbies," Camille nodded and
chuckled, picking up a forkful of sea bass. She had just
opened her catering and event-planning business in a small
warehouse space and had offered a series of cooking

The Scent of Lies

classes to start bringing in money and to meet potential new clients. Her idea worked brilliantly and it pushed her business forward to success. Those classes also brought this group of women together and they had grown to become best friends.

"My turn," Maggie said. "I remember that I took the class to learn how to cook somethin' other than my mama's down-home recipes," she told them, sprinkling a little dressing on her salad. "I had hopes of impressin' and snaggin' a successful man, but it hasn't quite worked out that way." Maggie offered a mock pout. She was still single, much to her chagrin, but her little boy had grown up and recently enlisted in the navy. She was now financially independent and providing only for herself.

"Evan and I were newly married," Emily recalled, "and I wanted to learn to cook for his sake. I was the worst cook ever and you really helped me, Camille. Of course, I was so bad it wouldn't have taken much to make me better," she admitted, which drew laughter from the other girls.

"And what about you, Isabel?" Camille asked.

Isabel set her burger down and cleared her throat while she wiped her mouth with her napkin. "Alex wanted me to take the class. He loves to cook and make all kinds of scrumptious things. With him being a lawyer and me working at the FBI, we both work pretty long hours. I took the class for him, so we could have fun cooking and creating dishes together on the weekends. It's hard to believe it was five years," she patted her tummy, "and fifteen pounds ago." A nervous giggle escaped her lips.

"Hey, wasn't there another woman in that first class with us?" Maggie asked.

"Yes, Abby something," Emily said.

"Abby Randall," Isabel replied. Her memory was sharp and clear. As a financial analyst, she had a habit of paying close attention to details.

"Yes, poor Abby," Camille said.

"What do you mean, poor Abby?" Emily and Maggie said in unison, then turned and grinned at each other.

"Oh, you haven't heard?" Camille sat up straight and leaned forward.

"Heard what?" Maggie's interest appeared to be piqued, obviously expecting a tidbit of juicy gossip.

"Now, don't tell anyone you heard it from me, but...she and Bob are getting a divorce." Camille leaned back a little, as if to let the information sink in.

"Divorced? Abby and Bob always seemed so happy," Emily commented. "I ran into them a few times around town. They seemed like things were going well. I wonder what happened."

"Well, I'm not one to gossip, but I ran into her one day at the mall and we chatted for a few minutes," Camille explained as she picked at her sea bass. "Abby had taken classes from me several times, so I knew her fairly well. She told me she thought they were blissfully happy and everything was going along beautifully. They have three children, you know, a nice home, and lots of friends—she said their life was perfect. Then one day, out of the blue, Bob told her he had fallen in love with another woman and he wanted a divorce. I'm sure it just broke that poor woman's heart."

The Scent of Lies

"How can that happen?" Emily asked. "I mean, how can you think everything is perfect and then out of the blue your husband doesn't love you anymore?" At the mention of Bob falling for another woman, her mind again went to the note she'd found. She just had to find out who Delia could be and how she was connected to Evan.

"Abby said he traveled a lot for work, so he obviously did whatever he wanted to while he was away," Camille surmised, "and then he pretended to be the perfect husband and father while he was home. I guess he must have gotten tired of pretending."

"Don't you just hate men like that?" Maggie asked with a scowl.

Camille's eyes lowered and her expression became sullen. "Now that I think about it, my Jonathan travels a lot for work too." Her gaze slowly lifted and her normally upbeat and carefree tone had dissolved. She sounded genuinely worried. "You girls don't think that sort of thing could happen to us, do you?"

"No, honey," Maggie replied, putting her hand over Camille's. "You need to stop talkin' like that."

"My word, you and Jonathan are perfect together," Isabel told her. "I don't believe for a moment he would do that to you, or your children."

"I agree, Camille. That's just plain crazy talk," Maggie added. "Don't you agree, Emily?"

Emily didn't say anything. She was caught up in her own thoughts, wondering if something like that could have happened to her and Evan. Like poor, unsuspecting Abby, Emily had thought she and Evan were blissfully happy too, but now she was having doubts. And if it could happen to her and Evan, it could also happen to Camille and Jonathan, couldn't it?

Even in the refreshing spring breeze on the open-air patio, Emily felt like she was suffocating under all the talk about unfaithful husbands, and she had to get out of there. "I'm sorry to cut this lunch short, ladies." She abruptly stood, pulled a twenty dollar bill out of her wallet, and laid it on the table.

"But you've hardly touched your lunch," Camille said in surprise.

"I need to meet those clients I was telling you about. I'll talk to you all soon." Emily dashed a quick glance behind her, leaving Maggie, Camille, and Isabel looking stunned and speechless as she hurried away.

As much as Emily regretted having to lie to her friends, she simply had to beat a path out of there. All that talk about *seemingly* happy marriages and *possibly* unfaithful men was more than she could stomach. After that conversation, she was even more determined to discover the identity of this woman named Delia.

At least it was true that she did have an appointment to show homes later that afternoon, but since she had a couple of hours to kill before then, she headed over to Evan's old office. One way or another, for her own peace of mind, she was going to find out if her late husband had been cheating on her.

The Scent of Lies

CHAPTER TWO
A Ring of Deception

EMILY PUSHED OPEN one of the large wooden doors and entered the lobby of the historic gray-stone building that sat on Main Street in the heart of Paradise Valley, a quaint, picturesque town situated just north of Boise, Idaho. After walking down a short hallway, she stood before the door to her late husband's office. The opaque window in the top half of the door still bore the lettering *Evan Parker, Private Investigator*.

Fighting with the key in the old keyhole, it finally gave in and unlocked. She pulled in a deep breath to steady herself before entering. She stood still for a moment in the doorway, surveying the dusty room. She had not been to this office since Evan's death. The murder had gone unsolved, and she had been left to wrestle with the unknown.

Her chest tightened and a thin sheen of sweat covered her skin as heart-wrenching memories came flooding back to her. Her feet seemed frozen to the floor and she was momentarily paralyzed by the visions. Evan had been found shot to death in this place, in the corner by the file cabinets, a single gunshot to the back of his head. The local police detective had no suspects and no prospects.

At the time, she had been told that the police had discovered a fat stack of cash with a rubber band around it in a locked drawer in his desk, totaling five thousand dollars. Since the money was still there, the authorities figured it wasn't a robbery, but it did cause them to wonder why he would have that much cash with him. Emily wondered too—on more than one occasion.

Since Evan had been shot at fairly close range, with no sign of a struggle, the police assumed the killer must have been someone he knew. They had questioned every one of his clients after finding their names when they searched his computer and the file folders in the cabinet.

The police had even suspected Emily for a time, as the spouse is often the first person they look at. After verifying her alibi, they all but ruled her out. She was having dinner with the girls at a restaurant at the time of the murder, but there was always the possibility, the detective had said, that she'd hired it done. He had suggested that maybe her paid killer posed as a new client that just hadn't made it into Evan's records yet.

In time, the police decided Emily probably had nothing to do with her husband's murder and the pile of cash was eventually released to her. So, with no real clues, old Joe Tolliver, the town's only detective, eventually gave up and filed it away as a cold case.

It wasn't that Paradise Valley could not afford to hire another detective, because it had grown into a largely

The Scent of Lies

affluent community. In the last ten years or so, it had become known for its million-dollar homes built along the Boise River, and there were an ever-increasing number of five- and ten-acre horse property subdivisions gobbling up the surrounding farmland.

The reason for having only one detective was simply that the mayor and city council members saw no need to waste the taxpayers' money. Paradise Valley hadn't had a murder in more than twenty years—until Evan was killed.

Focus, Emily ordered herself, remembering why she was there. Her mission was to find out who Delia was.

Sitting down at Evan's old metal desk, she rummaged through it, searching for anything that had this woman's name on it, but she came up empty. Then she went through all the folders in the file cabinet. Again nothing. She checked the calendar in his computer and even did a total search of the hard-drive for the name—still nothing.

Her eyes moistened and her throat tightened a little when she noticed the framed photo on the desk. It was a picture of her and Evan, smiling and snuggling in happier days. Picking it up, she lovingly traced his face with her finger. Her heart missed his sandy brown hair and piercing light blue eyes.

Emily spied the cross-directory phone book on top of the file cabinet and gently set the picture down. She grabbed the directory and flipped it open on the desk. Digging around in her purse, she found the slip of paper that showed Delia's phone number. She laid it down next to the book.

Scanning the pages as she ran her index finger across them, she located the number and read the name Delia McCall. The name sounded vaguely familiar. "Delia McCall," she muttered several times, but she couldn't place it. So she decided to be brave and dial the number. She needed to know this woman's connection to her husband.

The phone on the desk had been disconnected long ago, so she made the call from her cell phone.

"Hello." The woman's voice was low and sultry.

"Is this Delia?" Emily asked nervously.

"It is. Who is this?"

"This is Delia McCall?" Emily asked again, her heart thudding in her chest.

"Yes. Who is this?" the woman insisted.

"This is Emily Parker, Evan Parker's wife."

"Oh, Emily, yes, Evan mentioned you." Delia's voice changed to a lighter tone.

"Evan mentioned me?" Emily was stunned by her comment. She wondered why her husband would be talking to this woman about her.

"Yes, several times."

Emily slowed her breathing, hoping to get her nerves under control. "I have to know, Ms. McCall, what was your relationship with my husband?" She held her breath, waiting for the answer.

"My relationship? Well, I, uh…" Delia stuttered and stammered, obviously caught off guard. Was she hiding something?

"Well?" Emily pressed, irritated by the woman's evasiveness. If it had simply been a business relationship, why would she not just come out and say it? Emily had to

The Scent of Lies

ask what she was really wondering. "Were you having an affair with my husband?"

"What? Oh my, no." Delia laughed. "Is *that* what you thought?"

"Well..."

"No, Emily. Evan was doing some work for me, but it was supposed to be hush-hush."

"What kind of work?"

"I don't want to talk about it over the phone. Can we meet somewhere? I'd be more than happy to answer all of your questions."

"When?"

"Let's say this evening around eight o'clock, at that Moxie Java over on State Street?"

"All right," Emily reluctantly agreed. She wasn't sure why this woman was acting so mysteriously, but maybe she could shed some light on what happened to Evan.

Emily clicked off her cell phone and tossed it back in her purse. It would be best to get out of that office as quickly as possible before more memories came back to haunt her.

***

Emily drove home and grabbed her mail out of the mailbox on her way inside. On top of the stack of mail was a letter from the landlord of the office building that housed Evan's office. Tearing it open, she found a past-due notice stating she needed to pay the back rent plus a substantial late fee.

Her real estate commissions had been enough to keep her personal bills paid since Evan's death, but this extra fifteen hundred dollars a month for the office lease was putting an additional burden on her that she was having a hard time covering, especially since it sat unused. With Evan and his income both gone, her finances had increasingly become uncomfortably tight.

Kicking her shoes off, Emily grabbed a diet soda from the refrigerator and moved to the breakfast bar. She set the small pile of mail down and perched on one of the stools. Holding the past-due notice in her hand, she took a long drink of soda and glared at the words stamped in red—PAST DUE.

She missed her husband for a lot of reasons, but right now it was for financial ones. Wondering what she was going to do, her thoughts drifted to the single asset she knew she could liquidate, her ace in the hole, but she had hoped it would not come to that.

The asset was a three-carat, emerald-cut diamond ring that her grandmother had left her when she passed away a few years ago. Her grandmother had married well the second time, and the extravagant ring had been a gift from her husband. After his passing, his children from his previous marriage were left most of his large estate, but Emily's grandmother was able to keep their home and her jewelry.

Emily had been thrilled to receive the stunning ring before her grandmother passed on, but because the ring was old, the setting needed to be cleaned and the prongs tightened. So, she'd kept it safely hidden away until she could have it polished and perhaps re-set in a more modern

24

The Scent of Lies

setting. While Evan was alive it was never a priority, but things change.

He used to kid her about keeping the ring in a plastic artichoke in the vegetable drawer of their refrigerator. She'd tried to explain to him what she saw as the brilliance of it. The fake vegetable blended in naturally with the other items in the drawer, she would tell him. Plus, if there was ever a fire, the contents of the refrigerator would not burn. He said he understood, but he still thought it was silly, that she should have kept it in a safe deposit box at the bank.

Now that her husband was gone and her real estate business was suffering from the housing crisis, she thought about selling the sizeable diamond to a local jeweler. As much as she hated to think of parting with her grandmother's ring, she did need the money. At the very least, she should have it appraised to see how much it was worth.

Emily went to the refrigerator to retrieve it. She pulled out the vegetable drawer and there laid her prized faux artichoke, nestled among the fresh plump tomatoes and asparagus. She unscrewed the stem and turned it over in her hand, prepared to catch the ring as it slid out.

But nothing came.

"Where's my ring?" she cried in shock. She jiggled the artichoke, but it made no sound. She vigorously shook it upside down into the palm of her hand, but still no ring.

Who could have taken it? Her arms tingled as her chest tightened at the thought. No one but she and Evan knew it was in there. *When could it have gone missing?*

She tried to remember the last time she saw it. She hadn't checked on it since months before Evan died. *Evan—no, he would never have taken it and not told me...or would he? But there was no one else knew it was there!*

Her thoughts jumped to the stack of cash the police had found in his desk the night he died. Had he pawned her ring and that was what he got for it?

Heat crept up her neck and onto her cheeks. She broke out in a cold sweat as she slumped down onto a chair at the kitchen table. *Now what?* With the ring gone, how she was going to pay the past due office lease and the mounting expenses in the months to come? Her heart ached at the possibility that her husband may have stolen it from her. That was the last thing she wanted to believe, but it certainly appeared that way.

***

Emily strolled into the Moxie Java coffee shop at the appointed time. A handful of customers were scattered among the tables, but she was looking for a woman sitting alone. As she stood at the counter ordering her tea, she spotted an attractive middle-aged woman sitting in the corner at a table for two. She was impeccably dressed in a navy blue pantsuit with lustrous dark wavy hair down to her shoulders.

Emily paid for her drink and then headed toward her. "Delia?"

"Yes," the woman replied, tipping her head up to greet her. "You must be Emily. Please, sit down." Delia motioned toward the empty chair across from her.

The Scent of Lies

Emily sat and laid her large leather handbag on the floor beside her. Her stomach twisted with nerves and she fidgeted with her cup, wondering how the conversation would go.

"I recognize you from the lovely photo on Evan's desk." Delia took a sip of her latté.

"I didn't know about you at all, but I do appreciate your willingness to talk to me and answer my questions."

"I'm happy to do it. I just want to say how sorry I am for your loss."

"Thank you." Emily bobbed the teabag up and down before using the spoon to squeeze the water out.

"Don't you hate that phrase—sorry for your loss?" Delia continued. "It just seems so blasé. Evan was such a fine man and he died too early."

"I appreciate—" Emily started to say.

Delia held up her hand. "No, please, let me finish. I'm sorry for how he died and that no one has been able to figure out who did it so the matter can be put to rest."

Emily wished Delia had stopped after sorry for your loss instead of going on and on, which only made her feel awkward.

"Thank you for saying that, Ms. McCall."

"Please, call me Delia." She gestured to the rows of muffins and scones in the display case. "Would you like something to eat?"

"No, I'm good. I'd like to get right to it, if you don't mind."

"All right," she agreed.

27

"Can you tell me what Evan was working on for you?"

"You're very direct, aren't you? I like that," Delia said. "I'm a big fan of always speaking your mind. It's a sign of a strong and intelligent woman."

"Thank you, but I'm looking for answers, not compliments."

"Okay, I'll tell you." She glanced around the coffee shop, leaned forward, and lowered her voice. "I asked Evan to investigate my husband, Ricardo."

Emily's curiosity was sparked and she leaned forward as well, taking her cue from Delia to keep their conversation private. "What did you suspect your husband was doing?" she questioned, "if you don't mind my asking."

Delia looked around again before she spoke in a low, muted tone. "I own Heaven Scent, the company that makes the candles and lotions and things. Perhaps you've heard of it."

Emily nodded her acknowledgement.

"I believed then, as I do now, that my husband was embezzling money from my company. Not only that, but I think he's cheating on me."

Emily realized why her name had sounded familiar. She had heard it in the news recently because of the company's explosive growth and expansion in the area. "Do you think Evan could have been murdered because of what he was working on for you?"

Delia shrugged. "I don't know. He was killed before he could give me the photos and the information he had compiled."

The Scent of Lies

"If the police had found his folder full of photos and evidence, Detective Tolliver would have questioned you or your husband about it, wouldn't he have?" Emily asked.

"Yes, but he didn't," Delia replied, sitting back and sipping her hot drink.

Emily's gaze dropped to her hands folded on the table, considering what to ask next, wondering what else this woman knew. There had to be more to the story. There just had to be.

"What if your husband killed Evan and stole the files so he wouldn't be exposed?" Emily felt a sudden shortness of breath as the possibility sunk in. Might she have just discovered an angle that Detective Tolliver never had?

"I can't imagine Ricardo would be willing to do something so horrible to cover up his affairs and the money he stole."

"Even if it meant keeping him from going to prison?" Emily looked blankly past Delia, playing out the imaginary scenario in her head, envisioning those last minutes of Evan's life if Ricardo had been the one to come to his office that fateful night. This was the closest thing to a suspect or motive she'd had.

"Emily?" Delia called out.

At the sound of her name, she snapped back to the present.

"I can see those wheels turning in your head," Delia said, as if she had a way of looking inside Emily's mind. "Evan told me you had a good head on your shoulders, the tenacity to keep digging until you find something. Am I right?"

"I'd like to think so," Emily admitted, wondering where Delia was going with this.

"He also told me you had helped him with some legwork on a few of his cases."

"Yes, awhile back, before becoming a real estate agent." She had done more than just legwork, but she preferred to keep that secret. "I'm a little surprised he mentioned that to you. He generally didn't want people knowing I worked on any of his cases."

"He didn't go into any specifics or anything, just that he thought you were smart and driven—a bulldog for details, he said."

"I see," Emily acknowledged. "That sounds like something Evan would say."

"That being said, I have a proposition for you." Delia leaned back in her chair and folded her arms across her chest. "Would you consider taking over the investigation your husband began?"

"Me?" Emily gasped, her eyebrows darting up in surprise. "Oh, I don't know..."

"Now Emily, tell me the truth," Delia leaned forward now, locking onto Emily's gaze, "wouldn't you want to know if your husband was seeing another woman behind your back? Or if he was stealing from you?"

A little shiver snaked up her neck at the commonality and Emily had no choice but to agree with Delia. "Yes, I suppose I would want to know, but I'm not a private investigator." Emily laughed a little at the thought of it. Evan had tried to discourage her from becoming too involved in his business, and now here it was being laid at her feet.

The Scent of Lies

"Well, I say smart and driven is just plain that, smart and driven, no matter what profession you're in. I'm willing to pay you twenty-five hundred up front to see this case through, and if it takes you longer than a week or two, I am happy to pay more."

"Twenty-five hundred?" She could definitely use that money right now.

"Yes. I'm desperate to learn the truth about my husband," Delia said, "and I can see you're eager to learn the truth about yours."

She's got that right. Emily folded her arms on the table and looked at Delia for a moment or two before proceeding, giving some thought to what she would need to know in order to help this woman. "Explain to me then, Delia, what makes you think your husband is stealing from you?"

"My CPA found some anomalies in the books. We think he's siphoning off money from our company funds."

"And on top of that, you believe he's seeing another woman behind your back?" Emily asked.

"Yes, I'm almost sure of it. My husband is quite a bit younger than I am, you see, and he's very good looking—the classic tall, dark, and handsome type."

"What's his name?"

"Ricardo. Ricardo Vega."

"And what makes you think he's cheating on you?"

"He's often vague about meetings he's going to and he's evasive when I ask about them. Sometimes they're in the afternoon, sometimes in the evening. And occasionally he smells like perfume when he comes home. Something doesn't feel right."

"Couldn't there be any reasonable explanations for his actions?"

"There could be, if he wasn't so distant and defensive with me. I can't remember the last time we had—" Delia hesitated and dropped the volume of her voice to a whisper, "—you know, sex. There was a time when he couldn't keep his hands off of me."

"Have you asked him about it?"

"Yes, I've asked him straight out if there was another woman, which he adamantly denies. But he has good reason to lie. He knows I would cut him off financially if I ever found out he was cheating on me."

"What about the missing money?" Emily's voice was barely more than a whisper. "Have you asked him about that?"

"No," Delia replied, with a slight shake of her head.

Surprised by the answer, Emily's question slipped out in full volume. "Why not?"

"Shhh, keep your voice down, please." Delia's eyes flashed around the coffee shop. "I haven't asked because, if I get solid evidence that he's embezzling from my company, I want to have him arrested. If I'd asked him about it, it might have tipped him off that I was on to him and he could have slipped away with the money he's accumulated."

"Makes sense." Emily appreciated the woman's forward-thinking shrewdness.

"What else do you want to know?" Delia asked.

The Scent of Lies

"I think I've got the picture. Do you mind if I give you my answer in a few days? I need to spend some time thinking about this."

"The sooner the better, Ms. Parker. I've already lost six months."

"Yes, that makes me wonder, why didn't you just hire someone else to continue the case after Evan died?" It seemed odd that Delia would just let it drop and not pursue the truth with another investigator.

"I was afraid to—the timing was bad, with the company expansion and all. I didn't know who to trust. If Evan's murder had anything to do with his investigation, or if word leaked out about the embezzlement, it could ruin my business."

Emily nodded that she understood. "But if I decide to take over the case, this investigation would certainly move a lot faster if I had the photos and evidence Evan had already gathered on Ricardo."

"It absolutely would," Delia agreed, "but I have no idea what happened to them."

"I looked around Evan's office a little this afternoon and didn't come across anything with your name, or Ricardo's, on it. I didn't even find anything that even showed he was working for you or that you had paid him."

"That's because I paid him in cash, so there would be no paper trail."

"How much did you give him?"

"Five thousand dollars, in two payments—twenty-five hundred up front and then another twenty-five hundred the day before he was killed. He'd been working on the case for a couple of weeks and told me he needed to continue the investigation for a while longer."

That must be the five thousand in bills the police found in his desk. The detective thought Evan might have been into something shady because of that cash, but no. A wave of relief washed over Emily at the realization that the money hadn't come from the sale of her grandmother's diamond, either. But if Evan hadn't taken the ring, where was it?

Other Books
By Debra Burroughs

The Scent of Lies, Paradise Valley Mystery Book 1

The Heart of Lies, Paradise Valley Mystery Book 2

The Edge of Lies, Paradise Valley Mystery Short Story

The Chain of Lies, Paradise Valley Mystery Book 3

The Pursuit of Lies, Paradise Valley Mystery Book 4

The Color of Lies, Paradise Valley Mystery Short Story

The Betrayal of Lies, Paradise Valley Mystery Book 5

The Harbor of Lies, Paradise Valley Mystery Book 6

The Lake House Secret, Jenessa Jones Mystery Book 1

ABOUT THE AUTHOR

Debra Burroughs writes with intensity and power. Her characters are rich and her stories of romance and suspense are highly entertaining. She can often be found sitting in front of her computer in her home in the Pacific Northwest, dreaming up new stories and developing interesting characters for her next book.

If you are looking for stories that will touch your heart and leave you wanting more, dive into one of her captivating books.

CPSIA information can be obtained
at www.ICGtesting.com
Printed in the USA
LVHW041615071120
671038LV00022B/137

9 781475 222197